RIDING SHOTGUN

"This here's a great team!" West shouted above the roar of the stagecoach. "I picked each horse myself."

Tim was starting to reply when something happened to West's face. His right cheekbone vanished, taking with it his eye and part of his jaw.

As the report from the shot that killed West echoed through the canyon, Tim felt the ferocious impact of the second shot high in his left shoulder . . . *and the war for the mountain of gold was on*!

THE GOLDEN MOUNTAIN

WILL C. KNOTT

Charter Westerns by Will C. Knott

THE GOLDEN MOUNTAIN
RED SKIES OVER WYOMING
THE RETURN OF ZACH STUART
LYNCHER'S MOON (coming in August)

WILL C. KNOTT

THE GOLDEN MOUNTAIN

CHARTER BOOKS, NEW YORK

THE GOLDEN MOUNTAIN

A Charter Book / published by arrangement with
the author

PRINTING HISTORY
Berkley Original / August 1980
Charter edition / July 1984

ISBN: 0-441-29758-7

Charter Books are published by The Berkley Publishing Group,
200 Madison Avenue, New York, New York 10016.
PRINTED IN THE UNITED STATES OF AMERICA

1

TIM BOLTON MOVED RESTLESSLY in his chair as the argument at the bar intensified. Slade Parkhurst, the house gambler, was goading Amos Bruder, who rode shotgun for Wells Fargo. Parkhurst was a tall, swarthy man. His victim was a bandy-legged fellow, at least a foot shorter.

Tim was sitting at a small table in the corner quietly sipping his beer. He wanted only to wash down the dust of too many miles. He did not want to get involved. He compressed his lips and looked deliberately away as Slade crowded Bruder mercilessly.

The sharp sound of a face being slapped pulled Tim's attention back to the bar. Slade was smiling thinly at Bruder now, as a dark line of blood traced a path from one corner of his mouth. The gambler had succeeded finally in goading Bruder to action. Now it was up to Bruder to somehow survive what must inevitably follow.

Slade Parkhurst's lidded eyes were bright with controlled fury as he stepped carefully away from the bar. The patrons on both sides of the two men moved swiftly out of the line of fire. Parkhurst wiped the blood off his chin with the back of his hand, glanced at the fresh blood, then smiled wickedly.

"You're carrying a gun, Bruder," Parkhurst said softly. "I expect you'd better get ready to use it."

"I slapped you 'cause you deserved it, Slade," Bruder said, edging back.

Slade's eyebrows went up. "A mild disagreement and you raised your hand to me. You are scum, sir. I demand satisfaction."

"Go get him, Amos!" a voice in the back of the room called.

Someone else sniggered loudly. Everyone in the place knew Bruder had no chance at all to outdraw the gambler. Bruder glanced angrily at the one who had called out, then looked back at Slade. The gambler's thin smile had vanished. His reptilian eyes were still. He was ready to pounce.

"You can't make me draw, Slade," Bruder said. "I only said you was a good poker player. Maybe too good. But I ain't the only one around here thinks that. And that don't give you no call to keep on insulting me like that." Bruder took another step back.

"You have questioned my honesty, sir. I questioned your good sense—and your breeding. You saw fit to strike me." Slade glanced quickly about him, a malicious smile lighting his dark face. "The time for talk is over, I am afraid. Anyone with a mouth as big as yours sooner or later has to pay for it."

There was nervous laughter at that comment. Then the silence in the saloon deepened as everyone took another step back and waited for Slade to draw on Bruder. Tim glanced around the room. He saw the eager, glittering eyes, the tongues darting out of slack mouths to moisten dry lips. Faces were flushed with expectation, the lust for a killing showing nakedly on each countenance. Like a wolf pack waiting for the leader to lunge, Tim realized.

"Draw!" cried Parkhurst, his hand darting down to his holster.

But as Slade's gleaming Smith & Wesson cleared leather, Bruder flung up both hands.

"No, Slade," Bruder said, the sweat standing out on his ashen face. "No! I told you! I won't draw on you."

Slade appeared ready to shoot anyway. For a moment he hesitated, his bright gun leveled on Bruder. But the tension had broken the moment Bruder had flung up his hands. Suddenly the room was filled with scornful laughter.

Though Slade had no choice but to allow his lust for Bruder's death to drain from his eyes, his fury remained intact. He still demanded satisfaction. In three quick strides he reached Bruder and slammed his revolver around with brutal force. The blow caught Bruder on the side of his head. The sound of the heavy weapon crunching into bone was not a pleasant one. Flung sideways to the floor by the force of the blow, Bruder looked dazedly up at the still furious gambler. Blood oozed thickly from a deep gash over his right temple. Slade smiled. He took a step toward the downed man, obviously intent on placing a kick where it would do the most damage. Bruder raised his forearm in a feeble effort to ward off the blow.

Tim's chair scraped harshly in the suddenly still room as he got to his feet. "Hold it right there, Parkhurst," Tim snapped.

Parkhurst spun about to face Tim.

"Why not try me?" Tim suggested mildly as he strode into the center of the room. He pulled up a few feet from the gambler and waited, his knees bent slightly, his right thumb hooked casually over his gunbelt.

"This is none of your concern, stranger," Parkhurst said.

"Name's Tim. Tim Bolton. You said you wanted satisfaction. I don't have any seconds and I guess my manners don't match that lovely southern gallantry you been showing just lately, but I'm willin' to stand in for this good friend of mine."

"You don't even know the man. You're a fool to butt in like this, mister."

"Maybe," said Tim. "But I'm ready whenever you are."

The gambler looked quickly down at Bruder, then back at Tim. Uncertainty, then the first faint stirrings of fear showed in the man's eyes.

"Come on, Slade," Tim said quietly. "You were hot to use that pretty shootin' iron a minute ago. Here's your chance."

Parkhurst started to reply, then caught himself.

The gambler saw the eager eyes now focused on him this time. They were revealing the same lust for blood he had directed at Bruder only a moment before. Parkhurst squared his shoulders.

He was an extremely handsome man, with a thin aquiline nose, high cheekbones, a well-cared-for mustache, dark eyes, and a full head of dark hair. He was wearing a long, immaculate frock coat and tan trousers that followed closely the line of his calves until they tapered snugly about the instep of his highly polished boots.

Everything about the gambler gleamed. Yet to Tim the man was an abomination. He had seen too many fun-lovin' cowboys at trails end fleeced by men of this gambler's stripe.

With a shrug Parkhurst turned and walked back to the bar. "Later, stranger. Later. You'll get your turn. I promise you."

Once as a boy of eight Tim had witnessed a drayman flogging his horse unmercifully while the poor laboring brute tried frantically to haul an overloaded wagon out of a deep mud hole. The horse's eyes were starting from his head in terror, his muzzle laced with lather. Unable to stand the sight, Tim had broken away from his father, darted out into the street, and flung himself upon the drayman in an attempt to wrest the bullwhip from his hands. The drayman flung Tim headlong, but a moment later the fellow was on his back in the mud where Tim's father had knocked him, while a swarm of onlookers placed their backs to the wagon and pushed it out of the hole. Only then did Tim's father and the others let the drayman drive off.

Afterward, Tim's father had smiled proudly down at his son and said, *There's only one thing worse than a man who would beat a horse, Tim—and that's someone who'd stand by and let it happen.*

Tim spoke carefully, deliberately to Parkhurst's back: "I'm a good hand at poker myself, Slade. Any time you want a game, let me know. But you'd better make sure you keep both hands on the table—and your sleeves empty."

At this studied insult, Parkhurst's shoulders stiffened. The man placed both hands palm down on the bar to steady himself. He glanced at Tim's reflection in the bar mirror. The silence in the saloon was almost preternatural by this time. Outside in the street a horse clopped by briskly and a door somewhere upstairs in the building slammed.

"I know what your intentions are, sir," Slade said, turning slowly to face Tim. "But I repeat. Later. When I am ready. You see, I prefer to be dealing when the pot is full. I am sure you understand."

"Yes. Slade. I do. You're yellow."

Turning his back on Slade, Tim reached down and pulled the groggy shotgun up onto his feet. In a few minutes Tim had Bruder sitting up at a table, his head resting forward on crossed arms. Tim bent close to Bruder's battered skull. The entire right side of Bruder's face was encased in a dark shell of coagulating blood. Tim hoped the man's skull was not fractured. He straightened in time to see Parkhurst and two others stalking from the saloon.

"Someone get a doctor!" Tim called to the crowd of men staring at him. He saw someone in the back nod quickly and dart from the place.

With Parkhurst gone, those remaining in the saloon crowded about Tim, smiling and shaking their heads in admiration. Some clapped him on the back, while others reached out to shake his hand. Tim looked around at the beaming faces and felt only a shuddering disgust. Not a single one of these men had spoken up for Amos Bruder earlier. Each one had been willing to stand back and let Parkhurst do whatever he wanted with the shotgun messenger.

With a barely controlled fury that startled them, Tim moved swiftly through the jubilant ranks, pushing the men aside roughly, angrily—until he reached the street, where the pervasive smell of honest horse manure washed from his nostrils the stench of such men.

Tim was settling down to his supper in Ma Boyle's restaurant later that day when a thin, redheaded fellow entered the place, spotted Tim, then came to a halt before his table. He was holding a sadly battered bowler hat in one hand. He could not have been more than seventeen, and there was an eagerness about him, despite his woeful dress, that appealed to Tim. The boy was obviously in straitened circumstances, but he was not beaten yet.

Tim smiled up at him in greeting. "What is it, kid?"

"Mr. Bridger wants to see you."

Tim carefully, deliberately, cut himself a piece of steak. Chewing it, he glanced back up at the redhead. "That so?"

The fellow nodded.

"And who might you be?"

"Cass Terhune."

"Pleased to meet you, Cass."

"Thank you, sir. I'm pleased to meet you also."

"Good. Now, who the hell is this Bridger?"

"He's the Wells, Fargo agent in Placerville, Mr. Bolton."

Tim sliced another piece from his steak. "Tell Mr. Bridger where I am." He smiled at Cass. "But you better hurry. I'm almost finished with this steak."

The redhead acted as if he had been stung. Turning quickly, he clapped on his bowler and hurried out.

Tim smiled and went back to his supper.

It wasn't long before a tall fellow dressed in a well-tailored dark suit strode into the restaurant and came to a halt in front of Tim's table. He was wearing a black string tie that was set off by a white broadcloth shirt. His boots were elaborately tooled. Looking down at Tim from out of a quite humorless face, he did not remove his white, immaculate Stetson.

Tim ignored him as he dabbed at the last bit of gravy with a portion of a roll. Glancing up, he caught the man's cold eyes.

"I guess you'd be Mr. Bridger."

The man pulled himself up to his full six feet. "That's who I am. I happen also to be the sole agent in this territory for Wells, Fargo."

"Pleased to meet you," said Tim. He indicated an empty chair with a wave of his hand. "Sit down and join me in a cup of coffee."

Bridger seemed offended by Tim's casual manner as he dropped into the chair beside Tim.

"I want no coffee," the big man told Tim. "That's not why I wished to see you."

Tim pulled his coffee toward him and began sipping it. "Then why did you want to see me?"

"Do you have a job?"

"No."

"Then I'm offering you one."

Tim looked sharply at the man. "What kind of job?"

"Bruder's been seriously hurt. Since you were . . . courageous enough to intercede in his behalf, I felt it only just that you should be offered his job."

"To ride shotgun?"

"The pay is excellent."

"That so?"

"Five dollars a day and meals at every authorized Wells, Fargo station between here and California."

Tim sat back in his chair and nudged his hat back off his forehead. That *was* a princely sum, all right. What the hell was this guy shipping, anyway? And then it hit him. That Billings Lode, the one outside town about ten miles south. It had been paying off steadily for months, which meant a lot of dust piling up in the Wells, Fargo office.

"You've got a gold shipment ready to go. That it, Bridger?"

Bridger was obviously annoyed at Tim for using his last name. But the man let it go and shook his head emphatically. "Not at all, Bolton. But in days to come I'm sure we will have large shipments of gold, very large. Meanwhile, our morning stage will be leaving at six sharp, and I need a shotgun. The job's yours if you want it and think you can handle it."

Tim sipped his coffee. His money belt was not exactly empty, but it was getting there. He'd come to Arizona Territory to see what he could find in the ground. Still, he'd never dug much in his life and he wasn't overjoyed at the prospect of sinking everything into mining tools and then moving out into those mountains—not after he saw what so many others had found: dust, sprung backs, spavined mules, and in more than one case—Apache arrows. The hopeless, filthy prospectors he'd seen lounging on the board-walks or swilling booze in the saloons had done much in addition to cool Tim's enthusiasm. But five dollars a day just to ride shotgun. That did not seem right.

Tim looked carefully at Bridger. The man was not telling him everything. This stage run the next morning was not just another stage leaving on schedule in the cold light of dawn. But the pay *was* good and it offered Tim what he now realized he sorely wanted: an alternative to prospecting.

"All right," Tim said. "But I don't own a shotgun."

"You'll use Bruder's Greener. It's a fine weapon."

Bridger seemed very relieved. "Be at the depot at five A.M. and I will acquaint you with your duties." Bridger stood up.

Tim nodded. "Until then, Bridger."

Tim watched the man hurry from the restaurant. He didn't trust Bridger, but he'd let his money do the talking for him—and keep his eye peeled for trouble.

2

THE STAGE DRIVER'S NAME was Charlie West. He was a broad-beamed, red-faced man in his fifties, wearing blue homespun pantaloons patched in several places with yellow buckskin. A horn-handled buffalo knife protruded from one boot and the polished butt of a .50 boot pistol from the other. A faded velvet-trimmed jacket topped by an ancient and very dusty sombrero completed the man's uniform.

He had been waiting for Tim to show up, and now in the dim, predawn light just outside the Wells, Fargo office, he looked Tim over carefully. Apparently satisfied with what he saw, he sent a black dart of tobacco juice out of the corner of his mouth. "So you're the one taking Bruder's place, hey?"

"I thought Bridger might have told you that by now."

"He told me."

"Thought he might've. He said something about Bruder having a Greener."

"He had one, all right."

"Where is it?" Tim asked.

11

"In the office."

"What's going out this morning?"

"A whiskey drummer, a mail sack, and a strong-box." Charlie spat again.

"What's in the strongbox?"

"Valuables."

"That's not being very specific, Charlie."

The driver frowned. "There ain't no gold in it, if that's what you're askin'."

Tim nodded curtly and looked the stagecoach over. Even in the dim light he could see that the coach was in excellent condition. The body was a bright red, the leather of the front and rear boots black and gleaming, the wheels' yellow spokes and narrow rims still shining from their recent waxing. The brake shoe looked hardly worn, in fact.

Tim looked back at West. "This is a new coach?"

"First run's today," West replied proudly. "They been working on it all night to get it ready."

Tim looked back at the gleaming coach. Was Bridger so anxious to sign him on just to protect this bright new stagecoach? He found it a possibility, but one difficult to take seriously. Tim had visited a few saloons the night before and had picked up an undercurrent of talk about an upcoming gold ship-ment, confirming his earlier suspicions. Fear that Bart Talbot and his gang would rob the assay office—so the talk went—had prompted Wells, Fargo headquarters in San Francisco to direct Bridger to ship out whatever gold he had by the earliest possible stage.

Tim looked back at Charlie West. "That strongbox up there. You put that up there yourself?"

The driver's face went cold. "Hauled it up there myself."

"You wouldn't mind if I checked it out, would you?"

West sent a long dark stream of tobacco juice from his mouth, then tipped his head, indicating that Tim could check out the box if he wanted.

"Never mind," said Tim.

"Next time you call me a liar, bub," West drawled softly, "you better be ready for a whuppin'."

Tim smiled. "I'll remember that."

"You been hearing that whiskey talk—about a gold shipment. That it?"

"In just about every saloon I visited last night."

"Should've got some sleep instead. That same story's been kicking around for months. Nothing to it. Nothin' at all."

Bridger appeared in the office doorway. "It's getting near that time, West. Shouldn't you be seeing to them horses?"

West glanced up at Bridger, a cold light in his eyes, and let loose a stream of tobacco juice that splattered loudly on the first step leading up to the office. Then without a word in response to his employer, he turned and walked off through the graying light toward the horse barns.

"In here, Bolton," Bridger said.

Tim moved up the steps past Bridger and into the office. The thin redhead was standing in the middle of the room. He was holding a Greener and a box of shells.

"That my Greener?" Tim asked.

The redhead nodded quickly and handed the shotgun and the shells to Tim. He seemed inordinately anxious to be rid of the weapon and the box of rounds. Bridger was settling in his chair behind his small desk.

"Here's a couple of day's advance on your salary, Bolton," the agent said. He shoved ten silver dollars across the top of the desk toward Tim.

Resting the Greener in the crook of his left arm, Tim collected the ten dollars and dropped the coins into his pocket. "Much obliged, Bridger."

Bridger waved off the thanks. "Wait'll you hear what I got to tell you first. We just got word that Shriber's station was hit by Apaches late yesterday. All that's left is a chimney and some pretty poor looking corpses that used to work for Wells, Fargo. Naretena's renegades, more'n likely."

Tim nodded. He'd heard about that Apache the night before.

Bridger pulled out a gold watch, glanced at it, then looked back up at Tim. "West should be pulling out soon, Bolton. I suggest you check out your weapon and give the man a hand."

Nodding briskly, Tim hefted the Greener, turned, and left the office.

It was Sheriff Cal Turner, Tim saw, who was personally escorting the whiskey drummer to the stage. Leaning over Tim, West watched impatiently as Turner helped the inebriated salesman to climb on board the coach. The drummer, his white shirt stained and his collar detached, lost his derby hat the moment he stuck his head into the coach. The sheriff picked it up off the ground and passed it in to the man. The drummer was effusively grateful. He shook the sheriff's hand, then leaned back and disappeared from Tim's sight.

The sheriff looked up at them. He was a blockily built man with broad, beetling brows, and features that seemed somewhat squeezed together. At the moment the man's small dark eyes gleamed with surprising malevolence. "You two better take good care of my friend here," he told them.

"Where we're goin'," drawled West, "the poor sonofabitch'll have to look out for himself."

"Why don't you ride along, Sheriff," suggested Tim, "seeing you're that concerned."

"Do I know you?" Turner snapped.

"Tim Bolton, Sheriff. Pleased to meet you."

"He's the one faced down Parkhurst yesterday, Sheriff," West drawled, "while you was out carousin' with your friend there. Now stand back or you'll get yourself a mouthful of dust."

"You talking to me, West?"

"I said stand back!" demanded West, as he turned back around and fitted the ribbons about his thick, gnarled fingers. "We got a run to make!"

The sheriff stepped hastily back out of the road. West—letting go a long rope of tobacco juice that narrowly missed the sheriff—took his foot off the brake and yelled "Hiyup!" to his team. The six horses broke into a trot, and the stage rocked on its fore and aft springs and rolled out of town toward a blood red streak of light gleaming in the slate sky.

Three hours later, the sun was a blazing ingot burning a hole in the back of their necks. Tim and West were covered from head to foot with alkali dust, their eyes peering through slitted lids at a cruel, brass-yellow world of sandblasted rock and desert. There had been no peep out of their single passenger since leaving Placerville, and neither one of them had bothered to check on the fellow. Since he was the only passenger, he was probably stretched out, oblivious to the world he was passing through as he slept off his drunk.

Abruptly the stage slammed down a twisting grade that led between two towering rock pillars. The stage rocked on through them and almost at once the horses began a straining climb up a twisting grade that had West flicking his reins constantly.

As the stage climbed higher and higher into the rocky fastness, Tim found growing within him a grudging admiration for the rugged, wild beauty of this fantastic land of towering monuments, twisting canyons, and walls of sheer, polished rock. This particular badland had been labeled the Devil's Playground, and Tim realized now how apt the name was as he peered about him at the shimmering, hunched creatures of rock that met his gaze on all sides. From their twisted, gargoylelike shapes he had no difficulty at all in imagining them to be souls congealed forever into attitudes of awesome torment.

"Keep your eye out," West grumbled, breaking into Tim's thoughts. "We're comin' into Apache country."

They came to a sudden downgrade and West slammed his booted foot onto the brake, keeping it there. At the bottom of the grade, Tim saw ahead of the stage the crooked crack of a dry wash opening across the road's twin ruts. He shifted the Greener in his lap nervously as the stage rocked on toward it. West hunched forward almost eagerly as he tightened his grip on the reins.

"Steady there!" the stage driver called to his horses as they neared the rim of the wash. "Keep on goin', damn you!"

The six horses plunged down the rough side of the wash. The stage seemed to pause on the rim before plunging crazily over it and struck the gravel sitting in the bed of the wash with a roar. The front wheels recoiled. The rear wheels skittered to one side, and for a moment Tim was sure the stage was going over. But the horses did not falter as West shouted to the leaders, urging them on with a scalding mixture of endearments and blasphemies. The horses lunged up the far side of the wash, their powerful muscles bunching, their hooves sending soft clods of dirt flying. In a moment they had gained the rim, and a second later the stage was out of the wash, lunging after them.

With a pleased grin Charlie West turned to Tim, the ribbons dancing in his hands as he pulled his horses to a more leisurely pace. "This here's a great team," West shouted above the roar of the coach. "I picked out each horse myself."

Tim started to reply when something happened to West's face.

The man's right cheekbone vanished, taking with it his eye and a portion of his jaw. As the report from the rifle that killed West echoed above the rattle of the stage, West's remaining eye lost its focus. The man dropped his reins and tumbled backward off the box.

Tim did not hear the second shot above the sound of the stage; but at almost the same moment that West lost his balance and dropped out of sight, he felt a ferocious impact high on his left shoulder. He was slammed back against the coach. The Greener slipped from his hands. He reached out to grab the baggage rail. By then the horses were bolting, the reins well down among the traces. The stage picked up speed precipitously and began to rock wildly along. Unable to hold on, Tim slipped over the side.

The whiskey drummer's head was out the window. The man was yelling something up at Tim. The last thing Tim remembered before he struck the ground was the look of pure astonishment on the drummer's face. Then Tim struck the hard-packed ground, landing on his shoulders. But it was the back of his head that absorbed most of the shock. Lights exploded deep within his skull, and he lost consciousness.

Naretena, cradling a gleaming Winchester in his arm, stood erect on the ledge high overhead, watching impassively as first the stage driver, then the shotgun messenger toppled from the stage. The powerfully built Apache chieftain was dressed in a long buckskin shirt, his buckskin breechclout hanging over his belt fore and aft. He wore a clean white headband to keep his thick lustrous black hair in place and on his feet were the traditional Apache moccasins, the *n-deh b'keh*, thigh-length, thick-soled, button-toed footgear that enabled the Apache warrior to cover 70 miles a day on foot. The Indian's face was typical of the Mescalaro Apaches—broad and rather flat, except for the dark blue eyes and the sharply prominent nose, legacies from a fierce Spanish grandmother whose voice had always carried great weight in tribal council.

Behind Naretena, on a ledge about six feet lower, a line of silent warriors waited. All but two of them carried bright new Winchesters. The remaining two, the youngest, carried the traditional weapons of the Apache—a rawhide sling, elmwood bow, and deerskin case, and the nine-foot-long war lances tipped with steel blades. The bows had a lethal range of 100 yards and their slings were capable of hurling stones at least fifty yards farther. All eighteen of the warriors watched their chief with eager, impatient eyes. They were like hounds straining on their leashes.

Naretena went down suddenly on one knee and using his rifle for support leaned far out over the ledge to see more clearly. What he saw caused him to grunt softly in appreciation.

He got back up onto his feet, turned to his war party, and waved them ahead of him off the ledge. He followed swiftly, silently, his Apache moccasins leaving no trace.

Tim awoke with the impatient cries of men ringing in his ears—that and the sound of boards splintering.

He was lying face down. Raising his head slighty, he saw the wrecked stage about fifteen yards farther down the road. One wheel had shattered on a huge boulder, and the whole stagecoach was leaning crazily on its side. Four men—Bart Talbot's gang, Tim had no doubt—were swarming over it. The whiskey drummer was lying spread-eagled on his back a few feet from the stage. His head was turned so that Tim could see his face clearly. There was a neat hole under one eye. The man stared glassily across the sun-blasted ground at Tim.

The horses had been set free. Tim could see them galloping out of sight down the trail. Looking cautiously behind him, Tim saw the body of Charlie West. The stage driver's body had shrunken, it seemed, under the pitiless glare of the sun. Tim glanced skyward. Already the buzzards were beginning to circle.

As Tim looked back at the men clamboring into the stage, he winced and almost cried out. His shoulder wound was growing more stiff and painful with each breath he took. But he missed the feel of hot lead burning in it. The bullet had passed cleanly through. With his right hand he examined the wound. It was not large. The bullet had torn through muscle and cartilage and might even have chipped the top of his clavicle; but the bone was not broken and nothing vital had been hit. He clenched and unclenched his fist and found he could still use his left hand. Yet every movement of the shoulder increased Tim's discomfort. Still, if he could cauterize the wound thoroughly and somehow stop the bleeding, he knew he would be all right.

Keeping his head low, Tim edged to the side of the roadway, then rose to his feet and darted quickly into the rocks. After waiting to hear if his movements had been detected, he peered around a boulder. From within the coach the sound of splintering boards still came. Occasionally a piece of floorboard came flying out the door.

At last the sounds within ceased. Tim saw one of the men leap down from the stage and race up a narrow trail. He returned a moment later leading four pack mules. As soon as the mules reached the stage, the men began jumping down from the coach, carrying at least two gold ingots in their hands. Swiftly the men packed the ingots into the large, padded leather *aparejos*.

The explanation was obvious to Tim. Bridger had hidden the gold under the new coach's floorboards the night before, which explained his desire to hire a new shotgun messenger for this run. It had not been as casual a run as he had tried to let on.

Tim looked about him. In a moment one of the men would glance over and notice he was no longer lying in the roadway. He inspected the rocky slope behind him and realized he could reach the bluff overlooking the canyon if he was careful. Using the boulders for cover, he made his way to the slope and started up. At times the footing was treacherous. On more than one occasion Tim found himself forced to flatten himself against the face of the rock wall and inch his way along until the trail widened. Meanwhile Talbot's men continued to loot the stage, the sounds of their jubilant progress coming up to Tim clearly in the thin air.

He reached the bluff with his mouth as dry as a bone, his chest heaving from the exertion, his shoulder on fire. He thought of all the calves he had branded during roundup and wondered if the white hot brand that seared each calf's flank had hurt as much as this shoulder wound.

He slumped down in a small patch of shade and closed his eyes for a moment to get his bearings, resting his head back against a cool boulder. After awhile the sounds of horses hoofs clattering over stone far below aroused him, and he made his way to the lip of the bluff and glanced down into the canyon. The four outlaws were leading the pack mules down the road. Two riders were at point, the others riding drag. As Tim watched, they left the road and started down a narrow canyon that appeared to strike deep into the heart of the badlands.

Tim pushed himself wearily to his feet, checked his sixgun, and started to trot along the ridge after them. The outlaws' heavily-laden mules would keep their pace down. And that meant Tim might be able to stay with them until nightfall. Then maybe he could move in on them.

It was at best a forlorn, desperate hope—but Tim clung to it with grim determination as he forced himself along.

3

AS CLINT ANDERSEN RODE he studied Bart Talbot's face.

Clint had ridden with Bart for two years. So far it had been a profitable partnership for them both. Oddly enough, Bart looked like a store clerk, not an outlaw. He had a long horse face, teeth that crowded out of his mouth, a receding chin and watery eyes. Yet at times Clint and the others had seen this ugly face lit by the fire of pure madness. Speculating on this now, Clint became certain that it was the knowledge of Bart's possible derangement—lurking just below the surface—that controlled Clint and the other men.

Clint cleared his throat.

Bart glanced swiftly at Clint. "Out with it, Clint. What's eatin' at you? That shotgun, still?"

"He was gone when I looked back, Bart. West was still on the road and so was the drummer. But that shotgun was gone."

"All right, then. He was gone. Now forget it. That only means he crawled off into the rocks to die. You saw him get hit."

Clint looked back at the trail ahead of him. What Bart said made sense, yet it did not settle him down any.

Abruptly he turned in his saddle. The skin at the back of his neck was prickling. *Damn it!* He couldn't shake that feeling—that certainty. He had felt it once before. In Wyoming Territory. When that fool sheriff had tracked him all the way from Kansas, then took him at his campsite. That same feeling. Clint had ignored it then. But not this time. He couldn't.

Through narrow eyes he searched the canyon's rim. Someone could be up there now following them. And on foot. At the pace these mules were taking, there'd be no difficulty at all in keeping up. Clint squinted at the bright sky and for a split second caught the glint of sunlight on metal. A rifle barrel, perhaps.

Clint swung back around in his saddle and looked at Bart. "I'm going to ride back a ways and have a look see."

"Why?"

"I saw something."

"What?"

"Sunlight on a rifle barrel, maybe."

Bart's teeth protruded slightly as the man smiled. His eyes remained cold, however. And Clint saw at once that Talbot did not trust him. But then Talbot trusted nobody. That was how he had managed to stay alive for as long as he had. "You sure that's what you saw, Clint?"

"There's only one way to find out for sure, Bart. It won't take me long, and I sure as hell won't have any trouble catching up with you later."

Bart pulled his horse to a halt. "We're camping in Jones Hole tonight."

"You think you'll get that far?" Clint asked, pulling up as well.

"You heard me."

"Then I'll be there."

"If you ain't, we'll leave without you."

"I said I'll catch up with you. I just want a look see."

"All right, Clint. Go ahead. Have a look."

Clint turned his mount and rode back along the trail, passing the four mules. He nodded without speaking to Tom Wales and Lonny. In a moment he had ridden around a bend in the trail and found himself suddenly alone, the towering intimidating walls of the canyon lifting into the shimmering sky on both sides of him.

He kept riding for almost half a mile, his eyes searching for some trail that would take him to higher ground.

Tim had long since descended to the canyon floor and had done his best to keep Talbot's gang in sight. But slowly, relentlessly, the four men had pulled away from him and Tim was no longer confident he could keep up. Boots were for riding, not walking. Every step he took now was hellish punishment.

Tim pulled up and cocked his bared head. He thought he had heard something. He had. There it was again. The clink of iron on stone. A horse was being ridden along the trail ahead of him. The canyon wall hid whoever it was. Tim glanced to his left.

A sheer rock face met his gaze. He looked then to his right. On this side the slope was not nearly as steep. And it was pock-marked with boulders of all sizes, what remained of a fault that had long ago split the mountainside and left this debris in its wake. The rocks would give him, he realized, the cover he needed. He scrambled up the slope and kept going until he found a huge boulder balanced precariously on a small nipple of cap rock. Wind-driven sand and rain had worn the rock's base to such an extent that it appeared to have no more than six inches in contact with the cap rock. And yet the monstrous boulder towered at least twenty feet into the air.

Tim ducked behind the rock and placed his shoulder against it. He felt the rock give some. But only a little. He looked around for a lever and saw a long dead limb from an overhanging bristlecone resting in a crevice and pulled it out. It was thick enough and as heavy as iron. A perfect crowbar. Then he cursed violently to himself.

The exertion had reopened his shoulder wound. He could feel the warm blood coursing down his chest and back. He sat down quickly as a sudden dizziness caused the slope to spin alarmingly around him.

You'd better forget that crazy idea, he told himself. *Just keep your ass down!*

Dropping the branch, Tim peered out from behind the boulder. The rider was still not in sight, but the sound of his horse's hooves on the stony ground echoed and reechoed off the walls of stone that towered on all sides of them. The rider appeared at last and Tim was pretty sure it was one of the outlaws, though the distance that separated them was at least a hundred or so yards. Something had brought the man back and Tim wondered what that might be. Could it be that Tim had been spotted trailing the outlaws?

The rider had on a fringed deerskin shirt he wore outside his Levi's. His hair hung down almost past his shoulders from under the black, low-crowned Plains hat he was wearing. When Tim saw the hat—and the powerful bay the man was riding—he came to a sudden decision. If he was going to survive, he needed that hat as well as the horse.

Swiftly he made his way down the slope, angling sharply to keep alongside of the rider. Every now and then the fellow pulled up and looked carefully about him, with special attention to the rim of the canyon above and behind Tim. When Tim had reached to within thirty yards of the outlaw, he cocked his revolver. In the silence of the canyon, the sound of the gun's hammer being pulled back echoed far— astonishingly far. At once the rider pulled up, peered almost directly at Tim, and reached into his saddle scabbard for his Winchester.

Tim stood up boldly then brought up his six-gun. He was astonished at how heavy the weapon had become since that morning. He steadied his aim with both hands and managed to squeeze off a shot. The round plowed a furrow in the slope less than ten feet away. A quick second shot was even less efficient.

By this time the outlaw had snapped the Winchester to his shoulder. Tim ducked back down behind a boulder a moment before the rifle barked. A piece of rock behind Tim disintegrated. Needlelike shards of stone peppered Tim's back and neck. He peered around from behind the boulder for a third shot. But as he tried to steady his aim again with his left hand, his injured shoulder protested so strongly that he was able to squeeze off what was at best only a blind, desperate shot.

He never saw where the bullet landed. The outlaw's rifle cracked almost in unison with Tim's third shot. The bullet caught Tim's six-gun in the cylinder, smashing it from his hand. Tim looked down at his numbed fingers and was grateful to be able to count all five still intact. Then he ducked low as another round slammed into the slope behind him.

The outlaw was levering swiftly now, spraying the area with bullets. Tim kept his head down and tried to keep track of the number of rounds the fellow squeezed off. When he thought the man was close to having emptied his firing chamber, he started back up the way he had come. The outlaw sent a round into the ground just ahead of Tim, and then there were no more shots.

Glancing down the slope, Tim saw the outlaw slap the Winchester back into its sling and unlimber his six-gun. At once Tim rose to his full height and scrambled frantically up the slope, aiming for the rimrocks he had been crouching behind earlier. The outlaw fired a couple of times at Tim, then gave it up and hauled his horse around. Tim could hear him urging his horse as far up the slope as he could manage to drive it. At last the fellow dismounted and started after Tim on foot.

When Tim finally threw himself down behind the huge boulder where he had sought refuge before, he knew that that crazy idea he had had not so long ago was now his one remaining chance. He glanced down the slope and saw the outlaw climbing swiftly toward him and realized he did not have much time. He snatched up the heavy branch, fitted it under the boulder, then lifted. The boulder rocked some. But not enough. Not nearly enough.

Tim glanced down the slope. The outlaw was much closer. Tim put his right shoulder under the branch and heaved a second time. The boulder rocked forward slightly, then returned to its original perch. Tim heaved up on the branch again. The boulder seemed to lean further this time. Tim caught on. He had to impart a continuous rocking motion to the boulder. Timing his thrusts now, he heaved upward again and again. Abruptly, he realized that he was not going to be able to dislodge the boulder with only the leverage he could impart with the branch.

Dropping the branch, he leaned his bloody shoulder against the boulder's massive side, waited for the right moment—when the boulder was beginning its forward momentum—and heaved. The blood thudded wildly in his temples. His cheek tucked against the cold, unyielding surface of the boulder, he glanced down and saw the dark stain that now covered his shirt front and most of his left thigh. He let go. The boulder rocked back on its tiny purchase, then lurched forward again. One last time, Tim flung himself against the boulder— and this time he felt it pause—hesitate almost, like something alive. He bent quickly, snatched up the thick branch and thrust it well in under the boulder, bent his knees, then ran in under the branch and straightened himself, straining mightily, throwing into his last heave every last ounce of strength he had left in him.

The boulder rose out of its tiny saucer of rock, trembled for a moment on the saucer's lip, then with a grinding, crunching sound began to roll. His head light from the exertion, his heart pounding, Tim let himself collapse headlong after it. On the ground, Tim saw the outlaw—less than fifty yards down the slope and directly in the path of the boulder—glance up in sudden dismay. The boulder struck a ledge and bounded almost lightly into the air, then came down heavily upon an upthrust of rock, shattering it to bits.

Dust and debris filled the air as the boulder thundered
on down the slope, smiting into atoms everything in its
path.

Tim saw the outlaw scrambling frantically to one
side. He was too anxious. He slipped twice. Each time
he got up he was more terrified than he had been the
moment before. Now he was uncertain which way to go
as other, smaller boulders, dislodged by the first,
bounded toward him, spreading their contagion to
everything else on the slope that could be uprooted and
swept before it. It was a furious avalanche by the time it
reached the outlaw. Tim saw the man go down as a
small boulder knocked one leg out from under him.
Then the boulder—its progress shrouded in great
clouds of dust—swept on over the outlaw, obliterating
him with ruthless finality.

From out of the great cloud of debris, the boulder
plunged with startling swiftness. With tremendous,
rolling bounds it reached the canyon floor, thundered
across it and smashed into the wall opposite,
disintegrating into great jagged chunks with one
fearsome crunch. The dust began to settle. A dark
swath had been cut in the slope. Tiny rivers of loose
sand still crawled toward the canyon floor and little
stones could be seen bouncing on down the slope until
finally even this motion was gone and there was
nothing but an awesome silence hanging over the slope
and the canyon floor beneath it.

Tim stood up. He could just make out the outlaw
lying on his back, spread-eagled. Reluctantly Tim
made his way down the slope until he reached the dead
man. It was not a pleasant sight: a great hand had
swatted him as efficiently as a barkeep would have a fly
crossing his bar. Tim looked beyond the broken body

at the outlaw's horse in the canyon below him. The animal had bolted a quarter of a mile farther down the canyon and was now quietly cropping grass in a shady spot.

Tim reminded himself how much he needed that horse. It should be carrying a canteen and a bedroll—in addition to that Winchester. Recalling then why this bloody piece of flesh at his feet had gone to his six-gun, Tim frowned back his distaste and bent to examine the man's gunbelt.

He was pleased to find that it contained at least fifteen undamaged rounds of .44/40 shells he could use in the Winchester. Tim stripped the belt off the dead man, then looked around for the man's revolver. He was not so lucky with this: the six-gun was at the bottom of a small depression, its barrel smashed flat. The outlaw's hat Tom found some distance from the body. He whacked the dirt from it, then punched it back into shape and put it on.

Without another glance back at the broken body, Tim scrambled down the slope toward the horse. He tried diligently not to notice the leaden shell of dried blood that extended from his left shoulder down past his waist. By now, the reopened shoulder wound was like an enormous, throbbing tooth Tim found himself wishing he could somehow extract.

Well, maybe later.

4

MOSES KELLY WAS CURIOUS but careful. He ducked down behind the boulder as the riders rode on past. Only when the sound of their hoofbeats had become but faint echoes among the rocks did Moses move out and continue up the trail.

The old prospector had recognized Talbot and his men instantly. Three of them, there were, all told—and four mules, heavily laden. Gold, most likely, from the way the four mules labored. The gang had finally raided the right stage, it looked like. But why in Sam Hill were they taking the gold into Diablo Canyon?

Mose's eyes suddenly lit as he answered his own question. The gang was stashing it, they were. The old man looked back at the canyon's narrow entrance. There was no longer any sound coming from the shadows. The place was as still as death.

He let the excitement that had momentarily galvanized him fade and looked back up at the trail ahead of him. His cabin was a good five miles away, and he knew the girl would be frightened if he did not arrive back by sundown. Besides, tangling with Bart Talbot's crew was a plumb foolhardy notion, and he was surprised at himself for even considering it.

He reached his burro and stowed his pickax aboard the patient beast, took up the reins, and began leading the pack animal across the rocky ground at a steady, ground-devouring pace. At seventy-three his once proud six-foot-three frame had shrunken noticeably, but he knew he could still keep pace with an Apache brave and outlast any white man half his age. He was wearing a ragged sombrero, a patched buckskin jacket, buckskin pants and, instead of boots, a pair of thigh-length Apache moccasins—a gift from his Apache friend, Naretena. His long beard was completely white, except at the chin where tobacco juice had stained it a rich mahogany.

As he hurried along he wondered if Naretena knew what Bart Talbot and his gang of cutthroats were up to in Diablo Canyon. Then he chuckled hoarsely. Of course Naretena knew what was going on. There weren't nothing that took place in this here sun-blasted wasteland that that redskin didn't know about.

Astride the outlaw's big bay, Tim watched the prospector hurrying along the trail below him. The man was more than a mile distant, yet Tim was tempted to turn about and overtake him. About a mile back, as Tim approached what he now realized was this miner's shack, he was driven off by two warning shots that came from the rocks surrounding the place. Before Tim turned his horse aside, he caught a glimpse of a pale, frightened face at the shack's single window. Watching now the old miner's swift progress across the bleak landscape, Tim realized that this old man could not have been the one who had fired those warning shots.

Then who had fired them?

After dragging himself up onto the outlaw's horse earlier, Tim had found little water left in the canteen hanging from the saddle and had been forced to search for water. He had found a scummy water hole sunk deep in a rocky basin. He filled his canteen, drank deeply of the gritty, red-tinged water, then examined his wound carefully. It was already festering, he found. Fortunately, a search of the dead outlaw's warbag rewarded him with a tin of sulfur matches and a knife. Tim built a fire, heated the blade in it, and cauterized the wound. The pain of it caused him to cry out. But the cauterizing effectively stopped the bleeding and made Tim hopeful it had halted the infection as well.

He had then rested ahwile before settling out once more on the outlaws' trail. It was curious, but the gang did nothing to cover their tracks. Pursuit did not seem to be worrying them, nor the fact that their four, heavily-laden mules were slowing them almost to a walk. They kept going deeper and deeper into the badlands, toiling across high, rocky ridges and then down through sweltering valleys baked by a blazing sun. More than once, glancing up at the fearsome eye staring down at him, Tim had thanked his good fortune in gaining a hat. As the day wore on, however, Tim had found it increasingly difficult to trail the gang through this seemingly endless, labyrinthine maze of canyons and towering mesas. He had soon become dismally aware that he was steadily losing ground to them.

• • •

Now Tim regarded the distant figure of the prospector thoughtfully. It was still not too late to go after the man. Perhaps the fellow might have caught sight of Talbot's gang. He was coming from the same direction the gang had taken. But even as Tim watched, the prospector disappeared behind a thrusting wall of rock.

Tim turned back around in his saddle and regarded the rocky trail ahead of him balefully. With a sigh he urged the bay on. He would just have to go on until he dropped from the saddle. There would be no help from anyone, especially not from an old bearded codger already well out of sight.

Two hours later, a little before dusk, Tim pulled up. Slumping wearily forward over the pommel, he gazed thoughtfully into the dark folds of the canyon that opened before him. Its entrance was narrow and twisting, the rock walls sheer and almost straight up. A cold desert chill was in the air now, but another chill—more ominous still—fell over Tim as he contemplated riding into that canyon after those three outlaws with night coming on.

He glanced up at the canyon's towering walls and saw two great horned projections of rock looming out over the canyon's entrance. They were like the horns of a cow or—better still—the horns of a devil. Tim tried to shake the persistent chill and decided to find a campsite. The bay was about done in and so was he.

Tim was certain the men were still in the canyon. For the last ten miles or so, one of the mules had been favoring his right front leg, slowing the outlaws' pace considerably and allowing Tim to catch up. The tracks were quite fresh now and there was little likelihood that the men would get through this canyon before dark. They were more than likely setting up their night camp in the canyon at that very moment.

Tim turned his mount off the trail and urged it down a gentle slope in the direction of a stream he had glimpsed a half mile back. Later, perhaps, he would find the strength to leave his horse and see if he could climb to the canyon's east rim. Wherever Talbot's gang set up camp, Tim would have no difficulty spotting their campfire.

Lonny watched the two men nervously. Bart had begun smiling the moment Tom brought up Clint again. Lonny winced. He knew that Bart had just about had it with Tom and his nagging insistence that they go back and look for Clint. Bart tossed the remains of his coffee into the fire.

"You still want to go back and look for Clint, huh?"

Tom shifted his feet nervously. "I could've sworn them were rifle shots I heard. Besides, now we got the gold cached, they ain't no reason why we can't go back for a look see."

"That's right. There ain't no reason."

Tom smiled in sudden relief. "Then it's okay? We can go back now and look for Clint?"

"Not we," said Bart. "You. You go on back and look for him, Tom. First thing in the morning you get on that sorry horse of yours and go find Clint."

"Me? Alone?"

"That's right. Alone." Bart's lidded eyes regarded Tom coldly, calculatingly.

Watching the two of them, Lonny felt suddenly nervous and went back to his Smith & Wesson. He had emptied the chambers and was in the act of inserting fresh cartridges when Tom had first approached Bart.

"All right, then!" Tom's voice was raised now in anger. "I'll do just that, Bart! I'll go back for Clint without you. But it sure is peculiar you don't want to join up with me and Lonny to go back after your friend."

Bart spat into the fire. "Clint ain't no friend. He's just a partner. Partner's are a dime a dozen. Ain't no man in this here trade's got a friend."

Tom hitched up his pants and looked over to Lonny for support.

"What do you think of that, Lonny?" Tom said. "Clint was sure enough *your* friend."

Even in the dim light cast by the flickering campfire, Lonny could see how Tom's long face had darkened in anger at Bart's response. But what concerned Lonny was the cold look in Bart's eyes at this moment. It sent a chill down Lonny's back. Lonny holstered his six-gun and looked at Tom. "Guess maybe we'd best forget about Clint, Tom. He's gone for good, seems like. He had no business goin' back alone like that. This place is alive with Apaches. Clint should've had better sense."

"Apaches? I ain't seen a one!"

"You never do, Tom. Not till it's too late, that is."

Bart smiled across the fire at Lonny, his lean features taking on an almost satanic cast. "Well, *hell*, Lonny!" Bart said. "I don't figure we ought to stand in Tom's way. Let him go back and look for Clint. There ain't no reason for us to stop him."

"Guess you're right, at that, Bart," Lonny said, walking toward the spot where he had stashed his saddle and the rest of his gear. As he passed Tom, he said, "Go right ahead, Tom. Find Clint if you want."

"Hey, now wait a minute," protested Tom. "I just

thought you'd be as anxious as me to go back after Clint."

Lonny hunkered down beside his saddle and began to unlace his soogan. "Don't know what put that idea into your head, Tom. Now what say you cut out this palaver. I want to get some shut-eye."

With a short laugh, Bart turned his back on Tom and headed for his own sleeping gear against the canyon wall. Tom was left standing before the fire irresolutely. He looked first after Bart then he turned to face Lonny.

"Lonny," he began almost plaintively. "I thought sure you'd be willin' to go back with me to look for Clint."

"Get some sleep, Tom!" Lonny said, his voice grating harshly. "Bart and me, we don't want to hear no more about it."

Tom's face went slack. With those words Lonny was telling Tom that he was throwing in with Bart. It was no longer Clint and them against Bart. With Clint gone, that neat plan they had settled on before the raise was as dead as a doornail. It was Bart's show now—all the way. And it irritated Lonny that Tom was too damn stupid to see that.

"You understand me, do you, Tom?" Lonny asked, allowing the exasperation he felt to show clearly in his tone.

"Sure, Lonny," Tom said dispiritedly. "I understand."

Tom turned and without another word walked over to his gear and slumped down beside it.

Lonny glanced across the flickering campfire at Bart. For a moment he thought he could see the man's eyes gleaming in triumph. It was not possible. Yet Lonny was certain all of a sudden that Bart had known

what they had intended all along. Lonny shuddered at
the thought and began tugging on his boots. Yes, sir,
this sure as hell better be his last raise with Bart Talbot.
His nerves just couldn't stand another job like this one.

Lonny's boots were off and he was removing his hat,
preparing to roll into his soogan when he became
aware of a fine cloud of sand drifting down from
overhead. Instantly, every sense alert, he reached for
his gunbelt and removed the Smith & Wesson from its
holster.

Someone was above him on the cliff. In the act of
climbing down, maybe. Lonny glanced up, but could
see nothing. The moon had not cleared the canyon's
walls yet and the darkness—outside the small circle of
light cast by the campfire—was profound. They might
as well be lying at the bottom of an inkwell.

Could it be Clint? Lonny wondered, his heart
leaping at the thought. Was he back, making his play
finally?

The possibility transformed Lonny. His mind began
to race. Clint's plan had been to wait until Bart stashed
the gold, then get rid of Bart. They knew Bart would
insist—as he always had—on taking half of the gold
and splitting the remainder between them. This time
the three of them had decided to change that pattern
for good, to split the gold only three ways.

So that could be Clint above him right now.

In fact, the more Lonny thought about it, the more
certain he became that Clint's going back to check on
that shotgun messenger had been only a ruse to enable
him to surprise Bart when the time came. Lonny
frowned with the intentness of his concentration. The
possibilities were occurring to him with a suddenness
that confused him. And alarmed him as well. Suppose

Clint had seen where they had stashed the gold and now intended to get rid of the three of them—Lonny and Tom right along with Bart?

What the hell! If Clint knew where they had hidden the gold, he wouldn't need any of them. The thought sent the hair on the back of his neck to prickling.

The sand was no longer sifting down.

Still clutching his revolver, Lonny glanced across the dying campfire at Bart and Tom. Both men were apparently asleep. Lonny looked up a second time at the wall of rock that loomed over him and decided to wait until the moon rose clear of the canyon wall before investigating.

There was a narrow game trail that led to the top of the canyon wall. It was one Bart and Lonny had noticed on their way back from the mine shaft. Lonny could climb to the canyon's rim that way and meet Clint—if he was up there. But what if Bart awoke and saw Lonny crossing the canyon floor to get to the trail? Lonny considered that for a moment, then decided he would just have to tell Bart he heard something and was going to investigate. Meanwhile, the thing now was: how soon would it be before Clint made *his* move?

His Smith & Wesson in his right hand, Lonny lay his head down and waited for the moon to light his way across the canyon.

Now that the moon had risen above his left shoulder, Tim could see the canyon floor below him almost as clearly as if it were daylight. The campfire had long since pinpointed Bart and his men. Now Tim could see their horses and the four mules. The mules he noted at once, were no longer carrying their burden. Somewhere in this canyon, then, the gold had been hidden.

Their mules and horses were grazing up the canyon on a small patch of grass that was almost blue in the moon's clear light. From this height the animals looked like sheep and the sleeping men but tiny dark smudges on the floor of the canyon.

Tim's shoulder was on fire—and the fire had spread. He was burning up with fever. It had hit him the moment he dismounted a few hours back. His knees had almost buckled. Since then, his weakness had grown steadily worse. He shook his head. It was hard for him to believe that as clean a hit as this could bring on this much grief and discomfort. But he realized now it wasn't the bullet: it never was, as his father had warned him so often. It was the damn gunpowder. Earlier, while attempting a descent from another spot over the outlaws' camp, he had almost passed out and had just managed to catch himself in time to prevent a headlong plunge into space. As it was, his frantic scrambling had sent enough loose dirt and debris down the slope to have alerted the gang had they noticed.

Tim felt somewhat steadier on his feet now. And he was certain he could negotiate this narrow game trail he had discovered. But it was what lay after that troubled Tim. When—and if—he captured this gang, he would have to lash each one of them to his horse and drive them ahead of him back to Placerville, on the alert every moment for any attempt on their part to break loose. Contemplating such a journey in his present condition back through those blistering badlands gave him the shudders. He saw no alternative, however, not if Wells Fargo was to learn where all that gold of theirs was hidden.

Tim started down the trail to the canyon floor. However, he was so intent on the narrow path ahead of him that he did not notice the dark figure far below stir himself and then dart swiftly across the canyon floor, heading for the foot of the same trail down which Tim was now moving.

Lonny paused and peered cautiously up the trail ahead of him. Someone was moving down the trail toward Lonny, the soft clunk of his boot heels coming to Lonny clearly in the silent night.

Clint?

Lonny ducked aside as the sound of the approaching footfalls grew louder. If it *was* Clint, Lonny realized, he sure as hell wasn't making much of an effort to keep quiet.

"Who you waiting for, Lonny?"

Lonny spun. Bart, his six-gun glinting menacingly in the moonlight, was crouching behind him on the trail.

"Hell, Bart," Lonny whispered frantically, "I don't know! I just heard something."

"Sure, you did. It's Clint, isn't it? You're going up to meet Clint."

"You must be crazy, Bart."

"You think I believed that cock and bull Clint handed me?" The man chuckled, his protuberant teeth bright in the moonlight. "You three been planning this for some time. And I been waitin'. Now just stand quiet. I want to see the look on Clint's face when he sees me here with you."

Fear—a cold, insidious knife—probed deep into Lonny's vitals. Bart was going to kill them both. He had been watching and waiting all this time. It was all the excuse he needed to cut Lonny and Clint out. He must have been glad at the thought of what they had been planning. At this realization, Lonny's despair gave way to a violent, uncontrollable anger. *The sonofabitch!* He had been playing with them all this time! Just like a coyote with a field mouse, only now this coyote was fixing to end the game.

With a barely audible oath, Lonny flung himself toward Bart. Before he reached Bart, the man's six-gun blazed and Lonny felt the powerful, sledging impact of the bullet as it slammed into his gut an inch below his belt buckle. In that instant he knew he was dead.

But his momentum knocked Bart backward off the trail, and as he felt the man going over under him, he felt a savage determination to take Bart along with him. If he was on his way to hell, he wasn't going to ride through them gates alone. Lonny felt himself bounce off a boulder, then became dimly aware of himself rolling and finally tumbling head foremost down the precipitous slope until—a few yards above the canyon floor—he became airborne.

He struck on his side and lay still for a moment, stunned. When at last he was able to stir, he lifted his head and saw Bart, on his hands and knees a few feet from him, trying to push himself upright. The man was shaking his head groggily.

The pain in Lonny's gut was awesome. It felt as if he'd left half his insides back up there on the trail. He sat up and looked down as calmly as he could at the hole in his gut. In the moonlight he saw his dark lifeblood pulsing from it and something white and glistening uncoiling steadily from within. The pain grew in intensity with each passing moment. Never had Lonny believed that anything could hurt this much.

He looked over at Bart and saw that the man was looking at him closely. As soon as Bart caught Lonny's eyes with his, he slapped at his holster. But it was empty; Bart had lost his gun the moment Lonny knocked him off the trail. Lonny smiled and pulled out his Smith & Wesson, aimed carefully through a clamoring haze of pain and pulled the trigger.

There was no report. He had forgotten to cock the hammer.

Concentrating, he did what he could to block out the pain and slowly cocked the weapon, dismayed at the enormous expenditure of effort it took now. But he was too late. Bart, standing over him by this time, kicked the six-gun out of his hand. Lonny winced and looked up at Bart's narrow face. Lonny had never realized until that moment just how much like an animal—a sly, cunning animal—Bart looked.

Bart drew back his right foot and aimed another kick at Lonny—this time at Lonny's gut. Then, as Lonny nearly lost consciousness from the pain and tried to crawl away on his torn belly, Bart walked over to where Lonny's gun had come to rest, picked it up, aimed carefully at the back of Lonny's head, and pulled the trigger.

At the moment of the bullet's impact, Lonny felt as if he had been kicked in the head; the force of the round drove his face into the ground and the rest of him followed as he plunged headlong into bright nothingness. . . .

Tim had heard the first shot, then the sound the two bodies made as they tumbled down the slope to the canyon floor. Scrambling down the trail a few yards farther, he watched the two men stirring back to consciousness after they came to rest. And now he watched as the tall, lean one lowered his smoking revolver and looked back up the trail. He seemed to be peering almost directly at Tim.

"I know you're up there, Clint!" the man yelled. "Get down here!"

Startled at the command, Tim drew back into the shadow of a rocky shelf. This was Bart Talbot calling to him, he realized. In some way Bart had become aware that Tim was on his way down the trail and was obviously mistaking Tim for someone else. What had caused the fatal quarrel between the two men, Tim had no idea. He was simply relieved to have one less outlaw to deal with.

He peered cautiously down into the moonlit canyon. He had no difficulty picking out Bart—and another one of the gang running across the canyon toward Bart, the dark outline of a six-gun in his hand. Bart swung around as the man got closer. Angry shouts echoed in the canyon. Abruptly the third outlaw raised his gun. He was too late. Flame lanced from Bart's own weapon and the outlaw staggered, managed to get off a wild shot, then crumpled to his knees. He had just enough sand left in him to raise his gun again.

Bart aimed swiftly and fired a second time. His last remaining gang member pitched forward. Tim heard the distant clatter of the man's six-gun as it struck the ground in front of him.

Bart swung around then and called up through the darkness, "Come on down, Clint! It's just you and me now. We can split it fifty-fifty. There ain't no hard feelings!"

Tim walked to the edge of the trail and stood silently, looking down. He did not know if Bart could make him out against the dark canyon wall. He waited. Shading his eyes, Bart peered directly up at him, then waved. Tim waved back. As Tim watched, Bart holstered his gun and started back to the campfire, certain he had struck a bargain with a man he called Clint.

Holding the rifle in his right hand, his finger on the

trigger, Tim made his way cautiously down the trail. By the time he reached the floor of the canyon, Bart was hunkered down by the campfire, fussing with the coffee pot. Flames brightened the campsite as Bart fed a couple of fresh pieces of wood to the fire.

Bart glanced around as Tim approached. He apparently saw nothing in Tim's appearance to alert him. At once Tim realized who Bart thought he was—and who "Clint" was. Clint was that outlaw Tim had killed earlier, the one whose hat he now wore.

"I suppose you been up there, watchin' us all the while," Bart said. "You know where the gold's hid, sure enough. That right, Clint?"

Tim knew that if he answered, Bart would know at once that he was not Clint. He did not reply and kept on walking. The flames from the reawakened fire lit the outlaw's lean, burnished face. The man's eyes were dark hollows.

"What's the matter, Clint? You holdin' a grudge 'cause I treated your two buddies to some lead soup? Never could see why you throwed in with them anyways."

Tim was within four yards of the outlaw when he caught the gleam of metal just under Bart's elbow—the barrel of his six-gun, its muzzle pointing directly at Tim. It moved as Tim approached, tracking him smoothly.

Tim stopped and tried to bring up the rifle and aim it like a revolver. But the barrel was too heavy. His left arm was practically useless now and he thought about dropping to one knee and resting the barrel of the rifle on his knee to steady it. He thought all this in an instant. At the same moment Bart's revolver fired, sending a long, lancing tongue of flame into the night. The bullet snicked his right sleeve.

Astonished, Tim found himself on one knee, attempting to bring up the rifle so he could rest it on his left knee. His right hand and the rifle and the rest of his body seemed to be in league against him. Nothing was really attached any longer. He heard the rifle clatter to the canyon floor and looked dumbly down at it. Then he looked up at Bart.

The man was standing now, his revolver extended, a look of pure astonishment on his face. Then his face passed into shadow as did his whole body. He loomed over Tim.

"Who the hell're you?" he demanded. "You ain't Clint."

Tim tried to answer. Only the enormous, leaden fatigue that bore down upon every muscle—upon every thought—made that impossible. He had been losing blood steadily, he realized, and this was the result. And the fever persisted. Despite the cold desert air, sweat was breaking out all over his body. It made no difference. He no longer had the strength to shiver.

Bart leaned closer. "I said, who are you?"

Tim tried to shake his head, but it was no good. He felt himself toppling sideways. Dimly, he saw Bart's eyes narrow in sudden comprehension.

Smiling, Bart holstered his six-gun, obviously no longer concerned about the possibility of Tim using his rifle on him. "I know who you are, mister," he said, "and where you got Clint's hat. His Winchester too, looks like. You're that shotgun." Bart moved closer, tucked his toe under Tim's left side, and kicked Tim over onto his stomach. He did it idly, without malice. Tim felt the cold stone of the canyon's floor against his cheek. Bart began poking Tim about the shoulder, searching for the wound. When he found it, Tim felt the pain as a distant memory. "Yessir," Bart said. "I knew I hit you. A little high, that's all. Glad I didn't botch that little chore. Wouldn't want it said that Bart Talbot couldn't get a simple job like that done. I pay my debts."

Tim heard him step back.

"But I guess I better make sure right now," the man said.

Tim heard Bart cock his six-gun. He waited. A voice deep within him nagged at him fitfully, telling him he should roll over—get away somehow, scramble to his feet and run. But he was so tired. The cold stony ground upon which he rested seemed to cradle him almost gently.

Bart gasped.

Tim did not understand. Then he heard the man's six-gun fall to the ground, clattering heavily. Tim made a desperate effort to turn over, but was only able to lift his head and look around.

Bart was standing with his legs apart, both hands clasped about the shaft of an arrow imbedded in his chest just below the solar plexus. He was straining mightily. There was a look of cold fury on his face. As Tim watched, the man sank to his knees, still tugging on the shaft. His hands were still holding it when he toppled to one side into the blazing campfire and out of Tim's line of sight.

Tim let his head drop to the canyon floor as Bart's sudden scream rose to fill the night. He was sorry Bart had not been able to get off his shot. A bullet would have been a quicker death than that granted by the inventive mind of an Apache warrior.

Bart's scream ceased abruptly and the sound of moccasined feet surrounded Tim. He felt himself lifted by small, strong hands. His eyes opened. He was looking up into the face of an Apache warrior. The man's dark, savage face told Tim nothing of his intentions. The Apache's black eyes were inscrutable as well, and not a muscle on his face twitched. Abruptly Tim was thrown over the Apache's shoulder. Tim was dimly aware of other Apaches on either side of him.

The Apache began to run with the seemingly effortless ease typical of the Apache warrior. Tim closed his eyes. Perhaps he would be dead before they reached the Apache encampment.

5

TIM'S FATHER WAS WITH him in the nightmares that followed. The man's full, lush shock of dark hair gleamed as it had when Tim was a boy, and his smile was as ready. They rode together across the Texas plains again, crowding through the big bluestems, the grass's seed heads slapping at Tim's face and neck, sending the tiny, burrlike seeks down his back.... Then his father was standing beside him, hefting the enormous Colt he always wore, his face impassive, his eyes gleaming like sunlight through chinking, while he aimed and fired at the tin cans sitting on the fence posts so far away. Tim watched the cans dance into the air and looked up at his father again, only to find that his father's face had vanished, his features washed clean from under the big Stetson he wore....

And over and over again Tim found himself running down that hard-packed, sun-blistered street toward the Cattleman's Saloon, the roar of the shotgun's blast hanging in the quiet afternoon air. As always, he never made it through the saloon's still-swinging batwings as strong arms caught him from behind and held him. He struggled wildly to be free, crying out futilely, pleading, begging, calling out his father's name. . . .

His mother was in the nightmares, too, sitting once again in the living room by the coffin, weeping, her small pinched face staring at him almost reproachfully as he stole into the dim, musty room to stand numbly by her chair. . . .

Though the nightmares gradually faded along with the gnawing pain in his left shoulder, they were replaced by a terrified sense that he was being tormented by a host of fiendishly resourceful devils. They forced evil-tasting brews down his throat. Long-stemmed pipes billowing with a strong, acrid smoke were forced on him and as soon as the smoke reached his lungs, the world went hag, and he arose to live in a dim, twilight world crowded with grotesque scenes and Apache warriors that danced before his fevered vision like painted dolls, after which he would sleep for what seemed like ages. . . .

On more than one occasion Tim found himself sitting across from an old Apache sitting cross-legged before him in his wickiup. The Apache was puffing on his pipe. His small, nut-brown face was a spiderweb of wrinkles, his white hair light and feathery. It lifted constantly in the hot wind that blew in the open doorway. As the Apache spoke, Tim glimpsed the black stumps of his few remaining teeth.

On each occasion the wizened old man said the same thing:

I have been with your father. I come now to tell you this thing. Listen with your heart or you will not believe. It was none of your doing that your father is now with his white eye friends on the other side. He did not want to wait for you that afternoon. Trouble yourself no longer about this. He knew what waited for him inside that drinking place. The blast of a shotgun spreads, as you must know. Do you understand?

Tim's head felt as heavy, as monstrously large as a mountain, but he managed, nevertheless, to nod to the Apache. The Indian's face screwed into a grin—the same grin that Tim seemed to have witnessed a thousand times—and his black eyes grew still larger as he bent close.

Do not blame yourself that you were not beside your father that day. You would have been struck down as well. That is why your father did not wait for you as he promised. Be content now.

I have been with him and I tell you this is the truth. Listen with your heart, One Who Moves Mountains, and mourn no more.

The last time the Apache spoke to Tim, he finished by extending to Tim the pipe he was smoking. As Tim tried to refuse it, others came then to hold Tim down. As Tim struggled to free himself, the medicine man's face drew closer. His old stump-toothed smile seemed to fill the dark interior of the wickiup. . . .

He was on the side of a mountain or canyon. It was night and a bonfire was sending tongues of fire high enough to scorch the moon. He was dancing around the fire with the Apaches, his tall, angular frame towering over the smaller, more solidly-built savages. Their powerful brown bodies gleamed in the fire, and within Tim a fever of excitement surged through his limbs, galvanizing him, causing him to shout with the others, to fling back his head and cry out to White Painted Woman and her son Child of Water.

In his madness he set upon a huge boulder, the Apaches at his side. He felt the boulder rock against his

shoulder. He strained mightily and found himself back
on that other slope, the outlaw Clint scrambling up the
slope toward him. Another thick branch was thrust
into his hands. He dug its end under the boulder and a
host of smaller but equally powerful bodies joined his
as the immense boulder groaned, rose from its perch,
then rolled ponderously on down the mountain slope,
disappearing into the darkness.

At once it was as though the entire mountain had
shifted under his feet. The air was filled with rock dust
and heavy clouds of dirt swirled around him. The
shouting of the Apaches rose to a shuddering pitch and
Tim found himself once again staggering around the
bonfire, painted faces glaring up at him in triumph, the
night spinning wildly around him until the moon and
the stars swung wildly out of orbit and he was falling,
falling. . . .

When at last he emerged from that strange land of
sick visions and wild dreams, he was taken out of his
wickiup and his horse brought to him—along with all
of his gear, including his Colt and Winchester. His
black plains hat was clapped onto his head as he was
helped up onto his horse. He sat the horse dizzily,
blinking in the bright sunlight and looking around him
at the mean wickiups, their brush sides patched with
stolen army blankets. The Indians watched him
impassively, but with a silent respect Tim could not
understand, the squaws and children keeping well
back, either in or behind the squat wickiups. A
long-nosed, fierce-looking Apache with surprising
blue eyes rode up beside him, the other warriors by his
side.

Without a word this Apache, obviously the chief,
took out a black bandanna, leaned over, and tied it

around Tim's head, effectively blindfolding him. Then both wrists were bound securely to the saddle horn, his feet bound as well to the stirrups.

Someone took his horse's bridle and Tim rode off, as best he could blindfolded, the three Apaches accompanying him. Through the night he rode, one Apache in front leading, the two others on either side. They said not a word, the sound of their ponies' hoofbeats the only sure sign of their presence. As he felt the fresh sunlight on his face finally, the blindfold was ripped from his eyes and his Indian guides galloped off.

Blinking painfully in the bright morning light, he peered ahead of him and saw that the horse was heading for the dark outline of a small cabin less than a quarter of a mile away. It was the old prospector's place. When he was less than a hundred yards from the cabin, a rifle cracked in the rocks behind him, shattering the early-morning stillness. In a moment the old prospector emerged from the shack. He was wearing pale long johns and was barefoot.

Out from behind him crowded a young, wild-looking female. The prospector spoke to her sharply. She disappeared back into the cabin. In a moment she returned with a rifle and handed it to him. The prospector took it from her and then walked to meet Tim.

As the prospector grabbed the bay's bridle a moment later, he glanced up at Tim, a look compounded of curiosity and respect on his face.

"Naretena sent you, hey? You are one lucky man, mister."

"Never mind that, old man. Cut me down."

"All in good time."

The prospector led Tim's horse to his cabin, handing his rifle to the girl when he reached it.

"Get me my knife," he told her.

She disappeared inside the cabin and returned a moment later with a large Bowie. With swift strokes the prospector cut through the rawhide binding Tim to his horse. Tim felt himself sway dizzily.

"I think maybe you better help me down."

The prospector stepped close. Tim dragged his right foot back over the cantle, then felt himself falling. The prospector tried to catch him under his arms, but Tim's weight drove the man to his knees and almost beat him to the ground. With a curse and a grunt, the old man straightened and lifted Tim upright. Beckoning with a nod of his head to the girl, he directed her to Tim's right side. She ducked under his right arm and between the two of them, they helped Tim into the shack.

There was a single large bunk in the far corner, another smaller one between the wood stove and the sink. The large bunk was made up neatly with a patchwork quilt and a pillow filled with straw for ticking. Tim looked at it almost hungrily. When he was close enough, they let him down onto it. He lay quietly for a moment, dazed, then looked up at them both and smiled.

"Thanks."

"Who are you?" the prospector wanted to know. Behind him the girl was reentering the shack carrying the rifle the prospector had put down when he caught Tim. She brought it to the old man while he waited for Tim's response.

"My name's Tim Bolton."

"What the hell you doin' out here? This is Apache country."

"I work for Wells, Fargo. Riding shotgun. I was shot off the stage yesterday. Apaches picked me up sometime later."

"Yesterday, you say?" The prospector's eyes lit suddenly.

"That's right."

"You sure?"

Tim frowned. No, he wasn't sure, at that. "What day is this?"

"Wednesday, I reckon."

"I was with the Apaches longer than I figured. The stage left Saturday morning, I remember."

"You was with them Apaches a lot longer than you figured, friend." The old man was smiling appreciatively now, the yellowed stumps of his few remaining teeth prominently visible. The girl was stealing up beside him, staring with wide eyes down at Tim. "You're the one they sent out with that gold shipment, ain't you—the one that braced Parkhurst?"

"Now, how the hell did you know that?"

"Friend, you been with them Apaches better than a month. I just came back from Placerville a week ago. There ain't talk about nothin' else but what happened to that shipment. Your body's the only one they ain't found yet. And what the Apaches did to Bart Talbot's body is still being debated."

"Debated?"

"Whether or not the sonofabitch deserved it, I mean."

"A month, you say."

The old man nodded. "That's what I said."

Tim closed his eyes and tried to understand. It occurred to him suddenly that he was no longer feverish. He was weak—as weak as a kitten—totally exhausted in mind as well as body. But his fever was gone and his shoulder—he reached over to touch it—was no longer as painful as an exposed nerve. Sore, it was, and that was all.

The Apaches had fixed him up—saved his life, more than likely—then tied him to his horse and directed him to this old man's shack.

"Figured it out yet, friend?" the old man inquired.

"Naretena. You mentioned something about Naretena sending me. What did you mean by that?"

The old man glanced at the girl. "Last spring he sent her the same way. Later on he came by and told me she was taken from a band of *rurales* who'd treated her poorly, so poorly that the evil spirits had come to live in her head. So he gave her to me."

"I see. You and Naretena are on speaking terms."

"That's right."

"Why?"

"That's my business."

"I'd like to thank him."

"You'll get the chance—if he figures you deserve it."

"But I can't figure why he didn't kill me."

"Me, neither. Unless you did him a big favor."

Tim was suddenly too tired to continue the discussion. Too tired and too confused. "Can I sleep?" he asked the prospector.

The man nodded and turned to the girl. She shrank away. The old man told her to throw a blanket over Tim. She obeyed swiftly. Tim smiled up at her, turned to the wall, and was soon asleep.

The heat in the cabin and the buzz of the flies—one of which was crawling about his nose—was what awakened Tim. He glanced at the single window. The sunlight was slanting in at a high angle. It was close to noon or past it. Tim's mouth was dry and he was hungry. No. He was ravenous. The girl was at the sink, scrubbing tin plates with an obsessive intensity. She was wearing a faded blue sleeveless blouse and a heavily-fringed, knee-length buckskin riding skirt. On her feet she wore clumsy-looking, ankle-high buckskin moccasins.

The door was pulled open. The brilliant sunlight almost blinded Tim. Then the old prospector filled the doorway as he looked in to see if Tim was awake. When he saw Tim stirring, he pulled the door shut and strode into the shack, heading directly for Tim.

"How do you feel?" the bearded prospector asked.

Tim heard the sound of ponies galloping off. "Better. Much better."

"Hungry?"

"I could eat those moccasins you're wearing."

The old man nodded briskly, turned, and went over to the girl. He told her to fix the venison stew they had supped on the night before. The girl nodded quickly and hurried to do his bidding. The prospector returned to Tim. His alert brown eyes were warm and friendly—if just a mite cautious.

"She's a good girl," he said. "It won't take long."

"What have you got to drink?"

The old man smiled and hastened to the table upon which an earthenware jug sat. He brought it back to the bunk, unstoppered it, and handed it to Tim. Tim sat up and took the jug and lifted it to his lips. What poured down his throat set off a conflagration that singed his tonsils and burned a fiery path to his stomach—then began sending warm feelers out to his fingers and toes. With wide, appreciative eyes, Tim handed the jug back to the prospector.

The old man chuckled. "Mescal. The best. A present from Naretena."

"That's some medicine, all right."

"My name's Moses Kelly."

Tim nodded. "And you know my name."

"Do *you*?" There was a sudden gleam in Moses's eyes. He knew something that Tim did not.

"What do you mean?"

"I just been talking to Naretena. He rode up with a few of his braves on a brand new pony. He was inquirin' after your health, he was. Seems he has a great deal of respect for The One Who Moves Mountains. That's *his* name for you, anyway."

Tim frowned. He was remembering something—an old Indian peering at him through the fever. He too had called Tim by that name. And there was something else, but the more he plucked at the memory, the faster it vanished. . . .

Tim leaned back. "All right. Maybe you'd better explain."

"Seems them Indians watched you roll the side of a mountain down on one of Talbot's men. Then they saw you drink a well they poisoned. After that, danged if you didn't manage to kill two more of them buzzards. Only when you was going to let Bart finish you off did Naretena take a hand. Anyway, it seems them Indians sure admire your courage."

"You say they poisoned that well?"

"That's what the devils did, all right."

"How the hell did they pull me through, then?"

"Naretena's got a pretty fair medicine man, mister. And they must've shot down quite a few eagles for the down poultice they probably used on your shoulder wound. The gunpowder started it to fester some, but it was the poisoned well that really did you in. You was a pretty sick brave, looks like." He stood back and regarded Tim almost like a fond child. "Naretena was laughing when he told me. He won a bet."

"They were betting on whether or not I'd make it. That it?"

"That's right. Naretena bet his Winchester you'd live and won one of his men's fastest ponies. He was on it just now."

"Nice."

"For you, it is. You're alive, Tim. And it's Naretena you got to thank for it."

The girl approached with a hot bowl of stew. Tim could see the pieces of venison floating in it. Juices came to life within his mouth. His jaw ached.

"I can sit at the table," Tim said, throwing back the blanket they had covered him with. He was still in his Levi's, but the blood had been washed out of them and they were as soft as down. He sat up, put his hand on his thigh, and looked at Moses.

Moses nodded. "Them squaws beat the blood out of them pants. And they didn't stop there. Nice and soft, ain't they."

Tim got up. The room started to spin. He reached out and grabbed Moses' shoulder. The man helped him across the room to the table and let him down gently into the rough chair the girl had hastily pulled over to it. A wooden spoon was placed down beside the bowl of stew and Tim immediately set to work on it. He could not remember ever being this hungry before.

Moses sat down across from him and ordered some coffee from the girl. Then he looked across at Tim, watching him eat with cautious eyes. Tim caught the man's wariness and wondered at it. He said nothing, however, and finished the stew. A glance toward the girl brought him more. He watched her as she lugged over the pot and ladled the steaming, mouth-watering stew into his bowl.

She could not have been more than twenty. Her skin was light where the sun had not reached it, her hair almost blond. She looked furtively out at him through pale blue eyes and was constantly, nervously pulling her long tresses back out of her eyes and snapping them over her shoulders. Her features would have been quite beautiful if it were not for the way she pinched her lips into a grim line and allowed a frown, constant and undeviating, to rule her expression. The overall impression she gave Tim was of a captured bird. He imagined that if he reached out and placed his hand over her heart, he would be able to feel it pounding wildly against her fragile rib cage.

He smiled to himself at the audacity of this thought. As she stepped back from the table, he was aware suddenly that he did not know her name. He looked at Moses. "You haven't yet introduced us."

"Call her what you want. I call her 'girl.' Seems to suit. She answers to it well enough."

As the girl reached the stove, Tim caught her eye and smiled. "Thank you," he told her. "This stew is delicious."

Her frown deepened. She turned quickly, flinging her long hair back over her shoulders, and went back to scrubbing plates at the sink. It was what she had been doing when Tim awoke. Tim looked questioningly at Moses.

He shrugged. "She likes to keep the dishes clean—very clean. And that ain't all. Look at the floor."

Tim glanced down. The rough, uneven floorboards, he saw at a glance, had been scrubbed until they fairly shone. Each knot in the wood seemed to glow, in fact.

Tim leaned back and looked over at the girl. "I'd like some coffee, Marylou," he called.

She glanced around swiftly and Tim saw a sudden shrewd awareness pass like a cloud over her face. He smiled at her.

"I guess that'll be your name from now on, Marylou," said Moses.

As she brought Tim the coffee, he wiped beads of sweat off his forehead and glanced at the old prospector. "It's pretty damn hot in here, old man."

"What do you expect? It's a damn sight hotter outside. The sod roof I hauled in here takes a lot of the sting out of that sun. Step outside and you'll see what I mean."

"My horse all right?"

"It's in the barn with my mule and the mare."

Tim looked around the cabin. The place seemed to lack nothing. Indian blankets were hung along most of the walls. There were a couple of huge trunks along one wall containing the man's clothing and bedding. Both trunks were open and what showed seemed of fine quality. The corner that served as the kitchen was well stocked with shiny, copper pots and pans and a wealth of other utensils. The wood stove gleamed. It looked almost new. The chairs and the table were factory built and solid. There were new panes of glass in the window.

"You must be doing very well," Tim remarked.

"I am that," the fellow admitted—somewhat nervously, Tim thought.

Tim could tell the prospector had something on his mind he was anxious to discuss with Tim. Tim sipped his coffee and waited.

Moses cleared his throat nervously. "I suppose you'll be wanting to go back to Placerville as soon as you can ride."

"I will."

He nodded, seemingly relieved. The thought that Tim would not go back to Placerville as soon as he could had undoubtedly been worrying him.

Tim wondered if this was because of the girl. Or just the cramped quarters in this cabin. No. Tim had an idea it was something else, something a lot more bothersome.

"Why are you so anxious to get rid of me, Moses? What are you afraid of? The Apaches?"

The old man nodded. "You was lucky once. You won't be lucky a second time."

"I'm going back to Placerville, Moses, but I'm coming right back—with pack mules and some help. There's Wells, Fargo gold out there—gold I was paid to protect."

The old man sighed. "That's what I was afraid of."

"Why?"

"I told you. The Apaches."

"I mean them no harm. They seem to respect me. And you get along with them just fine, it looks like."

"There's a reason for that."

Tim waited.

The old man took a deep breath. "It ain't for me I'm anxious," he told Tim. "It's for the girl. Me, I ain't going to live forever. And I've seen and done just about everything a man can, I guess—and live to tell about it afterwards. But if I want to take care of her, I'll need money. And when I'm gone she'll need it. Really need it. If you're poor and strange, they'll lock you up somewhere. If you're rich and strange, why then you're an eccentric—and that's just fine."

"So you want to be rich—for yourself and for the girl."

Moses nodded.

"What's that got to do with the Apaches?"

"About a year ago Naretena and his braves circled me while I was out prospectin'. I'd been busy pannin' a stream and was beginning to show real color when I looked up and saw them all around me. They was friendly enough. I guess they'd been watching me for some time, though I'd never even knowed they was in the vicinity till then. What they wanted was simple enough."

"To quit working the stream."

"That's right." Moses looked at Tim shrewdly. "But that ain't all." The old man leaned forward in his seat. "Naretena, he talked pretty good English for an Indian. And he made a deal with me. He'd supply me with gold dust, he said. All the gold dust I needed. He had a mountain filled with the stuff, he said. A golden mountain. Apache gold. He would let me keep part of the gold dust. The other part I would use to buy things for him and his men."

"Like rifles."

Moses nodded. "Rifles and ammunition. And everything else they needed to keep them going."

"How long you been supplying the Apaches, Moses?"

"About eight or ten months now."

"I thought you looked pretty prosperous."

"Of course I still prospect, to make it look like I'm getting the gold dust from a strike I made, and there ain't too many anxious to check it out by prospecting in the badlands—not with Naretena and his band on the loose."

"You don't mind helping Apaches?"

The old man moistened his lips. "I was wondering if you'd be taking that attitude."

"I asked you a question."

"No, I don't mind. They been fair with me and I been fair with them. The way I see it, this is the first time I've been able to deal with fellow human beings and not be scared out of my socks I'd be cheated blind sooner or later. You give an Apache your word, and he gives you his word, and there's no more argument."

Tim shrugged. He owed the Apaches his life. And Moses Kelly had done him no harm. He had no call to judge either parties in this deal. But that did not mean he should not return to find the gold Talbot and his men had cached. That gold belonged to Wells, Fargo—and as he had just told Moses Kelly, it was still his responsibility.

"I'm coming back after that gold, Moses."

"You know where it's hid?"

"I think so."

"In Diablo Canyon?"

Tim remembered the rock formations over the entrance to the canyon. Yes, like two horns, the horns of a devil. Diablo Canyon. He nodded to Moses. "That sounds like it, all right."

"That's Naretena's country, Tim. Dangerous to go in there. Naretena might figure that gold belongs to him."

"Did he indicate to you he knew where the gold was?"

Moses smiled. "He didn't say a thing about it. But what the hell does that prove?"

"If it's still there in that canyon, I aim to get it."

"That's a fool chance you're taking."

"I like to finish what I start."

Moses looked closely at Tim. "And all you want is to return that gold to Wells, Fargo. Is that it?"

"That's what I said."

Moses leaned back in his chair. Tim could tell the man was reordering a host of priorities. "Naretena's gone south," he said, "for a war council with Victorio."

"To join him?"

"I doubt it. But while he's gone, we could maybe sneak in there, an...."

"We?"

"You'll need my help to find Diablo Canyon."

"I can find it."

Moses shook his head. "You might think so now, and maybe you could if you had enough time. But you don't have the time. Think back. Think how many turnings there were, how many landmarks you can recall. You were a mighty sick tracker then—and you were following a trail. That trail's gone now. Completely."

Tim considered Moses's words. The old man was right. Tim would have difficulty, great difficulty, in finding his way back through that tortuous wasteland.

"All right then, Moses. We."

"Now, where in that canyon you figure Bart hid the gold. Do you know?"

"I know where they were when I found them. They hid it nearby, I figure. They weren't in that canyon that long. One of their mules was pretty lame, so they couldn't have got very far before nightfall."

The old man's eyes gleamed. "A lame animal ain't that hard to track, maybe. And there's a few abandoned mines in there, too." He looked shrewdly at Tim then. "Of course, I'll want a reward for my help—a percentage of the gold's value. You could speak to Bridger for me. Tell him how you need me to get back to that canyon before Naretena returns."

Tim considered. "There's just one thing."

"What's that?"

"You'll be dealing with white men in this."

"I know. It ain't exactly a prospect I'm looking forward to." He glanced at the girl. "But she needs . . . something better than this place—and soon. Maybe this is the chance I been waiting for. If Bridger gives me a decent reward, we can be on our way." He smiled suddenly. "Ever been to California, Tim?"

Tim smiled back at the man. "Not yet."

"That's where we'll head."

"All right, then," Tim said. "I'll speak to Bridger."

"Marylou!" Moses called. "Bring over them new glasses I brought back from town last time."

Moses unstoppered the jug of mescal.

"We'll drink on it," he said.

The girl placed the glasses down before them. They were heavy goblets of a dark wine color and gleamed handsomely in the light—a strange and welcome contrast to the rude interior of the cabin.

"Thank you, Marylou," Moses said, as he poured the mescal into the goblets.

Tim was not certain, but he detected something in the girl's eyes, a warm, almost eager light—as if in giving her a name finally, they had lifted from her soul some of the darkness that crowded in upon her.

Tim smiled up at her. The fear—naked and terrible—returned to her eyes and she backed hastily away.

Moses shrugged. "She likes you, really. But she's still afraid to like or trust anyone. Even me."

He lifted his glass. Tim lifted his as well.

"Here's to Wells, Fargo," Moses said, "And to The One Who Moves Mountains. Let's hope he stays lucky." He grinned. "And out of poisoned water holes."

As Tim threw the fiery liquid down his throat, he found himself looking over at the girl—at Marylou. She was watching him as well, her light blue eyes no longer narrowed with fear, the frown on her face barely perceptible.

Then the mescal hit Tim and his eyes misted. He coughed and when he looked again, Marylou had retreated back to the kitchen sink and was scrubbing the plates as furiously as ever.

6

CASS TERHUNE ALMOST DROPPED the broom he was using to sweep out the Wells, Fargo office when he saw Tim nose his horse into the hitch rail. Tim thumbed the black Plains hat off his forehead and leaned back in his saddle.

"Howdy, Cass. The boss in?"

"No, he ain't. He ain't here," the redhead stammered. Then he grinned. "Is that really you, Mister Bolton?"

"It's me, all right, Cass," Tim replied. "You tell Bridger I'll be in the Miner's Haven." He pulled the bay around and proceeded on down Main Street.

As he rode away, he heard Cass calling out to someone. Soon a few townsmen were following along beside him on the boardwalk. It was a small crowd by the time he swung off his mount and dropped the reins over the hitch rail in front of the Miner's Haven. The silent, watchful crowd parted for him and he shouldered his way through the batwings, glanced once around the interior of the place, then headed for the bar.

He had caught sight of Parkhurst playing poker at the rear table with the sheriff and two others. As Tim bellied up to the bar, a few men from the crowd outside spilled into the saloon. In a few moments his identity had swept through the saloon.

Tim ordered a whiskey and was pulling it toward him when he heard a chair behind him scrape loudly in the suddenly still place, the sound harsh and unsettling. Tim turned in time to see a squat, vaguely familiar figure stumbling across the room toward him.

Amos Bruder.

"You're him!" the man cried, his words slurring. "Tim Bolton. You took my place on that stage! I owe you a drink!"

"I was paid well," Tim said, moving aside to let the fellow up to the bar. "Ten silver dollars. I have them still. Let me buy you a drink."

"Thanks!" The man grinned broadly and looked around the room. "I was hoping you'd say that!"

The tension snapped as laughter exploded.

Tim slapped some coins down on the bar. "Whatever he's drinking," he told the barkeep.

The man nodded and reached for a bottle of the cheapest whiskey in his stock. Bruder draped an arm over Tim's shoulder. "I want to thank you, mister. I never got the chance—and it looked like the Apaches was never going to give it to me."

"That's all right, Bruder," Tim said. "You don't have to thank me."

"Hell, I don't!" The man slapped Tim soundly on the back. The crowd that had grown about the two of them edged closer. Eager eyes watched them. Some were obviously enjoying the sight of Bruder cadging from the big man who had rallied to his defense a month earlier. Others, however, were eyeing Tim cautiously and seemed openly suspicious of him.

Tim turned back to the bartender and ordered another whiskey. Bruder had by this time draped his right arm over Tim's shoulder. Slowly, gently, so as not to injure the man's feelings, Tim straightened to his full height and threw his shoulders back so that Bruder was forced to remove his arm.

For a moment Bruder seemed offended. The man frowned slightly and shrunk back a bit. Tim took his whiskey and held it up before Bruder. He smiled. "I've had a long ride, Bruder," he told the smaller man. "I guess it was longer than I realized. Think I'll go hunt up a room at the hotel. I'm glad you're feeling better."

Tim's words were spoken softly, as warmly as he could manage under the circumstances. Bruder relaxed at once and smiled.

"Hell, I'm drunk," the fellow said disparagingly. "Guess I've been drunk too damn much lately," he added, and many around him laughed at that frank admission. "But I ain't too drunk to know a friend when I sees one."

He said this stoutly, as if he were daring anyone in the place to contradict him. There were none who did. Both men tipped their glasses and drank on it. As Tim put down his glass, he noted the large welt over Bruder's right ear. The bandage must have been removed recently. The hair about the gash had been shaven off and was now only a short stubble. Bruder was lucky to be alive, Tim realized suddenly. He felt a sudden warmth for the little man who now wanted nothing better than to thank his friend. It did not matter that he was as clumsy in this as he had been in trying to extricate himself from Slade Parkhurst's taunts earlier.

Tim spilled two more coins onto the bar. "For my friend, Amos Bruder," he told the barkeep.

"Thanks, Tim," said Bruder, his drink-sodden face flushing with pleasure. His blocky figure straightened and he looked around with the air of one who has inherited great wealth. He was planning, obviously, to stand all his friends to a drink.

Tim smiled and pushed his way through the crowd, heading for the street.

"Hold it, Bolton."

Tim stopped and turned. Slade Parkhurst was coming toward him, a thin cigar in his mouth, a malevolent gleam in his lidded eyes. When he saw the look on Tim's face, he smiled brightly, ingratiatingly, and came to a halt.

"Just a word, friend," Parkhurst began. "I harbor no ill will, I promise you. In a moment of weakness I turned with violence on a fellow human creature. I deeply regret my actions of that day." The man rocked back on his heels. He was enjoying himself very much. "So I say, let bygones be bygones. And welcome back to Placerville." His glance now moved swiftly around the crowd, catching the eye of many whom Tim had noticed earlier regarding him with sullen suspicion. "Yes, welcome back to Placerville," Parkhurst continued. "You are, it seems, a lucky man—a very lucky man, indeed. Even more remarkable, you are a sole survivor."

The sheriff stepped out of the crowd then and joined Parkhurst. "That's right, Bolton. You're the only one left alive. The whiskey drummer and Charlie West are dead. The Apaches dragged what was left of Bart and his men to Shriber's burned out station. But you're fine. Just fine. You walk in here without a scratch."

A voice from the back shouted, "How do you explain that, Bolton?"

Tim ignored the remark and turned to continue on out of the place. But the silence had deepened, become more menacing. Sudden hostility beat upon Tim with the heat of a desert wind.

"What's the matter, Bolton?" inquired Parkhurst gently. "Can't you answer that?"

Tim looked back at Parkhurst. "There's no answer for your kind, Parkhurst, or that other jackal back there."

"You calling me a jackal, Bolton?" Parkhurst asked softly.

Tim squared around to face the man. "Is there anything wrong with your hearing, Parkhurst?"

The gambler held both hands up, palms out. "I refuse to take offense, friend." He smiled. "I am just sorry you see fit to return honest inquiry with invective. All of us here would just like to know how you were able to manage it, that's all."

Tim smiled then. "The Apaches," he said. "Naretena's renegades. They took care of me, treated my wound, saw me through the worst of it. They saved my life."

The crowd shrunk back from Tim.

Still smiling, Tim turned and started again for the batwings. Before he reached it, Bridger burst into the place.

"Ah, Bolton!" he cried. "Cass told me you'd be in here."

Then Bridger saw the crowd facing Tim, the contempt on so many of the faces. He looked in confusion back at Tim. "Is . . . anything wrong?"

"Everything's fine, Bridger," Tim replied.

Parkhurst turned swiftly on his heels and thrust himself back through the crowd toward his poker table. The sheriff followed, and the solid flank of onlookers broke up. A few angry, muttered comments still came from the rear of the room, however. Tim understood perfectly. No man who was a friend to the Apache was welcome to these men. But Tim felt no sorrow at the loss of their welcome.

"Why don't we go to your office, Bridger," suggested Tim, moving past the agent. "Then I want some sleep. It has been a very long ride."

"Of course, of course," the agent said, following Tim from the saloon.

As Tim settled in the chair by Bridger's desk, he found himself looking closely at the man. He had not judged the man correctly before. Bridger had lied to him—and to Charlie West—when he let Tim think there was no gold on that stage. Yet the man must have spent the night overseeing its placement under the floorboards. His ruse had been elaborate, going to the length, as he did, of selecting a brand new coach so West would not wonder at the sound of workmen hammering away in the night. They were just getting the new coach ready, he was able to tell West.

Dressed in his dark suit, his white Stetson still on his head, he presented a somber, almost melancholy appearance. Indeed, he seemed to have aged considerably since their last meeting. His hollow cheeks and curiously high cheekbones gave him an almost cadaverous appearance. Despite this, the man's lips were full, sensual. His hair he wore long, his dark eyes, set deep in their sockets, were large and brooding. His hands with their big long fingers were finely shaped.

They gave him a look of suppressed strength. Tim felt something he had felt before, a sense of suppressed desperation.

Bridger folded his hands before him on the desk and leaned forward, fixing his somber gaze on Tim. "Well now, Bolton," he said. "You must have quite a story to tell. I'll want full particulars, of course, to wire the company's headquarters in San Francisco."

At that moment Cass appeared in the office doorway. When he saw the two of them at the desk, he pulled up sharply.

Tim smiled at the excited boy. "Hi, Cass. Looks like we found each other, all right."

"Get back outside, Cass," Bridger told the redhead. "And keep anyone else who wants to come in outside as well. We do not want to be disturbed."

Cass left in almost as great a hurry as when he entered.

"Once more, Bolton," Bridger said. "Your story, if you please...."

Tim told Bridger everything as he remembered it. He kept very little back and finished with Moses's offer to help them find Diablo Canyon and the gold hidden within it.

Bridger leaned back in his chair, a thoughtful frown creasing his forehead. After a few moments he took a deep breath and looked closely at Tim. "That is quite a story, Bolton. Remarkable, really. How do you account for the Apaches helping you like that?"

"That business where I rolled the boulder down on Talbot's man sure seemed to have impressed them."

"Yes. These savages admire courage greatly, I am told. And you say they believe it was you killed the other two."

"It was dark when they came upon us. I'm still

confused myself as to what really happened. I was half out on my feet by that time."

"And you say Moses Kelly knows where this canyon is? He can lead us directly to it—without delay?"

"Like I said—for a price."

"Yes. I should think so. I'll wire San Francisco. I am sure something can be arranged. Provided, of course, that we recover every ingot."

Tim shrugged.

"And you feel well enough to set out soon?"

"Is tomorrow soon enough for you?"

Bridger looked shrewdly at Tim. "How do you account for the fact that you recall so few details of the Apache encampment or their treatment of you? It sounds as if you were under the influence of some drug."

Tim considered a moment, then replied. "That's what Moses thinks, too."

"Laudanum?"

"No."

"What then?"

"Some Jimson, maybe, or peyote—if their medicine man's a Zuni. Moses thinks he might be."

"You've been missing for more than a month. All that time you were drugged?"

"Feverish from that wound, most of the time. Unconscious the rest. Whatever I remember is in bits and pieces. Nothing solid."

"Yes, well we must be certain to bring everything we will need then. And we'll have to be in and out of that devilish place as quickly as possible. I assume you realize that no one but us must know where we are headed. Or why."

"I've been thinking of that. And I've got an idea."

"I'm listening."

"I don't think I'm going to be very popular in this town come tomorrow. Looks like the best thing for me to do is take the stage out first thing in the morning. I'll get off at Twin Forks, purchase what we'll need, and meet you outside of town that night. I'll be camping in the breaks."

"Yes. I'll find a pretext for slipping away later that morning."

"Make sure you're not followed."

"How much will you need?"

"Enough for four good pack mules and supplies."

"I'll have it for you when you take the stage out tomorrow morning." He frowned suddenly. "I suppose we'll just have to assume that Moses Kelly is telling the truth about Naretena's band—that they have gone south to be with Victorio."

"It's his neck too if Naretena catches us in that canyon."

Bridger got up. "You'll have a ticket tomorrow morning, Bolton, and what cash you'll need. I'll leave the provisioning up to you. You said something about getting a room at the hotel. Do you need anything now?" The man was already reaching for his wallet.

Tim stood up also. "Thanks, but I still have most of that ten dollars you gave me."

The man frowned thoughtfully at Tim. "I'd say that ten dollars was a very good investment, Bolton—if we get that gold back, that is. Of course I don't need to tell you to be careful tonight. There are a lot of tinhorn heroes out there who can't abide Apaches—or Apache lovers."

"I don't love Apaches all that much, Bridger," Tim said. "But then they did save my life."

"Of course. Of course. I understand, Bolton. Just be careful, that's all."

"I will be," Tim said, starting for the door. "Don't worry."

As Tim led the bay into the livery stable, he was surprised to see his chestnut standing fat and sleek in the same stall he had rented for him better than a month before. His first thought was that he must owe Tompkins a sackful of silver for the animal's keep.

Simp Tompkins was cleaning out a stall when he looked up and saw Tim. He leaned the pitchfork against the side of the stall and hurried out, a wide, almost toothless grin on his face. It was a pale, gaunt face, the only color in it coming from his bright nose. It was close to a cherry red. Tim's immediate assumption was that swilling down booze was the only way the man could make shoveling horse shit for the rest of his life bearable. He was a stove-up cowpoke come to the end of his trail, and all that was left of the good old days was the clear, keen look in his bright blue eyes.

"I see you still have my chestnut," Tim said.

The man pulled up in front of Tim proudly. "I knew when they didn't find your body, you'd be back. You got the look of a feller that comes back. I was like that once myself."

"How much do I owe you?"

Simp frowned, then caught sight of the big bay Tim was leading. "I'll take that one in trade for the bill. And give you fifteen besides."

Tim looked back at the bay, then over to his chestnut. Simp was getting the best of it, but Tim didn't mind.

"Done."

Simp smiled and the two men shook on it. Then Simp led Tim over to the stall where his chestnut stood, stomping and swatting at the flies with his long tail.

"He's fat and sassy," Simp said, "just rarin' to go. I had quite a few offers for him, but like I said, I knew you'd be back for him."

"Thanks, Simp. Guess I'll unsaddle and take my gear over to the hotel. I wasn't here long enough the first time to find out. Where's the bathtubs in this town?"

"The barber shop, down the street. Two bits."

Tim nodded and went back to the bay, lifted off the saddle, and lugged it over to the chestnut's stall, dropping it astride the side of the stall. He took the saddlebags and the warbag with him as he crossed the street to the hotel. His room was on the second floor, overlooking Main Street. The Miner's Haven was directly across the street. For a moment Tim considered requesting another room, since sleep would be difficult with a wide-open saloon going full blast just outside his window.

Then he shrugged and dropped his gear onto the bed and went out to find that barber shop.

At first Tim thought the barber had simply made an honest miscalculation. But when he poured the second bucket of hot water into the tub, Tim knew that the barber—an enormously stout fellow with a large, fleshy, clean-shaven face, the cheeks hanging on each side in great dewlaps, and three vast chins—was deliberately trying to scald him. The man huffed stertorously as he stepped back with the still-steaming bucket. Except for a crescent of white hair at the back of his head, the man was completely bald.

"A little hotter the next bucket full," Tim told the man.

The fellow's eyes grew wide, almost bulging. Wheezing angrily, he waddled about and went for more hot water.

Tim was well lathered by the time the fellow returned. He was holding the bucket with both hands and was lugging it with great care, making sure not to splash any of it on his apron. The steam from it moistened his round, piggish face.

As the barber neared the foot of the tub, Tim rose up and with one quick movement reached out with both hands. His right hand grabbed the bucket's handle, his left the tuft of hair on the back of the man's bald pate. He wrenched down with his left hand and the man went to his knees, his head snapping back, his eyes staring up at the ceiling. Tim's right hand snatched away the bucket and dumped its steaming contents into the tub. At the same time Tim stepped out of the tub, lifted the barber by the hair, and before the man could cry out, ducked his head face down into the now scalding water and kept it there.

The man struggled violently, so violently that he pulled the tub over onto himself. Tim let loose and the man—squealing like a piglet on the run—staggered back and to his feet. He stopped squealing and began blustering. Tim threw him a towel. He snatched at it and wiped furiously at his round, pendulous face.

"You!" he panted wildly. "You almost drowned me! That water is scalding!"

"I know," said Tim. "Now right that tub and bring me more bathwater. The right temperature this time."

Two customers from the front of the shop had been drawn into the backroom by the barber's cries. They stood now in the doorway, lather still on their faces, astonished at the sight of the barber's beet-red face and

Tim's naked, lathered figure standing over him. The two other barbers pushed past them.

"This Apache lover giving you trouble, Matt?" one of the half-shaven men asked. He wiped the lather off his chin and took a step into the room.

"Never mind! Never mind," the barber insisted. "Get back to your chairs."

He looked fearfully back up at Tim as he spoke. He had felt the strength in Tim's arms—and the quiet rage as well—and wanted no further trouble from the man.

"It's all right, I said," the barber repeated. "I just had a little accident."

The four men turned and left the room. The barber waddled over and righted the tub. He picked up the bucket and hurried out to the boiler. As Tim waited, he wondered if he would be able to stay in this town much longer—let alone until the morning stage.

But he needed the sleep, damnit. And a good meal as well.

He compressed his lips angrily, determined that no matter what anyone in this town tried, he was going to get himself a double order of steak and fries and then a full night's sleep between clean sheets.

An hour later—his belly full, a toothpick stuck in one corner of his mouth—Tim entered the hotel lobby and started for the stairs. He heard his name called. Turning, he saw Cass hurrying across the small lobby toward him.

"Mr. Bridger told me to give you this," Cass said, thrusting an oilskin packet into Tim's hands.

Without another word Cass clapped his bowler onto his head and scurried from the hotel.

Tim looked around the lobby. The desk clerk was

watching him coldly. There was no one in this town, it seemed, that did not know by this time that Tim had been nursed back to life by his friends, the Apaches. That barber had been only the beginning; the waitress where he had eaten his supper had refused to look him in the eye and only his obvious impatience had made her wait on him when she did.

He had been a fool, he realized now, to have admitted to that offal in the saloon that he owed his life to Apaches. It had been an act of pure defiance his father would have understood—and deplored, for such arrogance always cost a man dearly.

It sure as hell had cost Tim's father.

Tim mounted the stairs and entered his room, locked the door, and quickly opened the oilskin packet. Two crisp one hundred dollar bills fluttered to the bedspread, also a small piece of paper with a note on it addressed to Tim. The note was short, its brevity emphasizing its urgency.

Bolton:
   It might be best if you rode out tonight. Here's the money you will need. I will meet you at the breaks tomorrow as planned.

                              Elias Bridger

Tim read the note twice, aware of a tightness growing within him. It was anger he was feeling, pure and simple. He did not like to be told what to do—especially by a mob of half-drunken miners and no-accounts. Tim folded the note and tucked it back into the oilskin packet along with the two bills, then placed the packet inside his shirt, nudging it down behind his belt. He walked over to the window then and looked down at the street below and at the Miner's Haven directly across from the hotel.

Night had fallen. The guttering gas lamps that lit the

street cast a lurid glow over the roiling crowd that seemed to have attached itself to the saloon's entrance. Men were shouting at one another in heated argument. Occasional shoving matches broke out. The crowd grew larger as more and more patrons of the saloon pushed themselves out through the batwings to join their friends. Men rode up, talked for a brief while with the others standing on the boardwalk, then hurriedly dismounted and slammed into the saloon.

As Tim was pulling back from the window, he saw someone emerge from the saloon, say something to the crowd, then turn and stride back inside. Everyone streamed in after him. Drinks were evidently on the house.

It was a lynch mob Tim was watching grow, and he knew it. He had seen such raucous, whiskey-fouled crowds before. And it was he they were after this time because, strangely enough, he had let the Apaches save his life.

Tim tried to understand. The Apaches had taken a bloody toll of miners prospecting in the hills around Placerville. They had done so for years. Naretena was only the most recent Mescalaro Apache to lead his band of renegades against the hated White Eyes. There was probably not a miner in that crowd below that had not lost a friend or an acquaintance to an Apache lance or bullet. And yet, despite their depradations and the interminable efforts of the cavalry to flush them, the Apaches remained safe in their seemingly impregnable rocky fortresses.

But here was Tim—within reach if only the members of that mob could generate the courage needed to act. They were bellying up to the bar at that very moment, stoking up what courage they could muster.

Tim frowned irritably. *Where the hell was the sheriff?*

At once, however, the futility of that hope caused him to shake his head wearily and turn from the window.

He snatched up his saddlebags and the rest of his gear and left the room. He did not go down the stairs. Instead, he followed the narrow hallway to the rear of the building. There was a window at the end of the hallway. He looked out and saw the slanting roof of the hotel's stable just under the window. He opened the window and dropped to the stable roof, angled down to the edge of it, then dropped lightly to the ground.

Emerging from an alley entrance a block further down the street, Tim darted across Main Street and into another alley. In a few moments he ducked into the livery stable through the rear door.

And found himself staring into the twin bores of a double-barreled shotgun.

7

TIM HAD FOUND OUT where the sheriff was. It was Sheriff Cal Turner who was holding the shotgun.

"Don't act too sudden," the sheriff said, lifting Tim's six-gun from its holster and tucking it into his belt. "Just stand easy. I only want to make sure you don't get hurt. You might say I'm your Guardian Angel."

"You look just like an angel, Sheriff."

Tim caught sight of Simp Tompkins then. The hostler was lying in an empty stall, sprawled on his side atop a pile of moldering hay. A whiskey bottle was clutched in one hand. The way the hostler was hunched about it, he looked like an incredibly wrinkled old baby curled up in a crib with his bottle.

"I mean it, Bolton," the sheriff replied blandly. "I'm marching you out to the town lockup and putting you behind bars for safe-keeping. It ain't safe for you to be walking the streets of Placerville."

"Then let me ride out, sheriff."

"Nope. Wouldn't hear of it. That mob wouldn't allow you to ride out of town tonight."

"I had not planned on leaving with much of a hurrah."

The man smiled and shook his head. Then he waggled his shotgun, indicating that Tim should precede him out of the livery and into Main Street. "The jailhouse's on the corner past the Miner's Haven. You just walk right on past them angry townsfolk and trust me."

Tim looked closely at the sheriff, actively considering an attempt to wrest the man's shotgun from him. The sheriff took a cautious step back as he measured the desperation in Tim's eyes. He waggled the shotgun a second time.

"Don't try anything foolish, Bolton. If this shotgun goes off at this range, it'll just be my word that it was you I shot. Of course, they'll love me for it, make me a real hero."

Tim found himself staring down the bores. The sheriff was right. If that load caught him in the face at this distance, there'd be nothing left for anyone to identify. He would have to take his chances with that crowd, then—and with the twisted motives of this sheriff.

Tim walked past the man and out through the livery's big stable doors onto Main Street, the sheriff following along behind him. Every once in a while the man would nudge the small of Tim's back with the barrels as a kind of reminder. Soon Tim was close enough to the Miner's Haven for some of the crowd to take notice of him and the sheriff.

A cry went up, and then another. The crowd broke toward them. As the men ran, their heavy riding boots made an ominous thunder on the boardwalk. That sound mixed with the shouts and strident curses flung at Tim caused a shudder to pass through him. The mob's mindless rage beat upon Tim with the force of something palpable.

He pulled up. The sheriff strode around in front of Tim, a grin on his face. He was enjoying himself. As the crowd streamed about them, he held up his left hand and kept the shotgun cradled in the crook of his right arm.

"Now, hold it!" the man shouted above the furious clamor. "This here man's my prisoner!"

There were hoots and laughter.

"What's he done, Cal?" someone shouted.

"Yah!" another cried. "What's the charge?"

"He let go in his pants!" came from the rear. It was a woman's voice, and a shout went up applauding that bit of humor.

The crowd surged forward.

"Let us have him!" someone shouted. "He ain't committed no crime! Let him go, sheriff. We'll take care of him for you."

"Maybe we'll carve him up a little, the way his friends carved up my partner last month!"

That cry came from the rear as well, but this time Tim caught a glimpse of the person who had spoken. He wished he hadn't. It was the face of a man transformed into something less than human by the hatred seething within him.

"Make way now!" the sheriff cried. "Let us through here. This shotgun's loaded. I don't want to have to use it. Not to save the likes of this Apache lover! Make way I said!"

Reluctantly, the crowd parted before them. Sheriff Turner reached back and pulled Tim around in front of him, nudging him forward none too gently with the shotgun. As Tim walked ahead of him through the crowd, he felt the spittle from those near enough to reach him. A few made clumsy efforts to grab him. A short man with a livid scar running from his eye to his mouth tried to kick Tim, but the crowd was too closely packed and his foot got tangled. He swore wildly in Tim's ear as he stumbled and fell back into the arms of those behind him.

The crowd on the boardwalk thinned, while another crowd formed in the street to keep pace with Tim and the sheriff. As they passed the Miner's Haven, the few left inside shouldered through the batwings to watch the parade.

Slade Parkhurst was the last through the batwings. He smiled when he caught Tim's eye. He seemed to know something that Tim didn't. He was filled with this knowledge, bursting with it. Nodding shrewdly to the sheriff, Parkhurst cast one more pleased glance in Tim's direction, then turned about, and disappeared back into the saloon. The few others who had come out followed him back inside.

Horse buns were flying by the time Tim and the sheriff reached the jail. Tim said nothing and simply kept his shoulders hunched, while the sheriff seemed close to losing his temper. The crowd, by this time, was enjoying itself hugely and seemed to take as much pleasure in deviling the sheriff as it did in threatening Tim.

Turner poked Tim harshly in the back as Tim stepped through the doorway into the sheriff's office and then with a shove sent Tim reeling across the room. Tim used his hands to brace himself when he struck the wall. Then he spun around to face the sheriff. Turner was closing the door. He glanced back at Tim, his face set, determined.

"You'll be staying here tonight, looks like," the man

said with a grim weariness. "Go on through that door. You can use the first cell on your right."

Tim nodded and walked into the cell block. The sheriff tossed Tim's six-gun onto his desk, picked up a key ring, and followed Tim. As soon as Tim entered the cell, the sheriff pushed its door shut and locked it.

Tim turned swiftly. "What the hell you locking me in for, Sheriff? I haven't committed any crime."

The man stepped back nervously as he peered in through the bars at Tim. "It's for your own good, damn it. If anyone breaks in, they won't be able to get to you. I'll have the keys."

"That's a lame excuse, Sheriff. And you know it. Unlock this cell."

Turner looked at Tim squarely then, his face reddening. "Who the hell do you think you are, giving me orders like that? You're in no position to be telling anybody what to do, mister. Damn you and your fool arrogance, Bolton! You deserve whatever happens!"

"And what might that be, Sheriff?"

Turner spun about and headed for the doorway. "I'll deputize someone to stay here with you," he said, pulling the door shut behind him.

A moment later Tim heard the street door open as the sheriff left his office. The noise of the crowd, which had kept at a steady level until then, swelled to a crescendo as the sheriff emerged.

Tim thought he could hear Turner shouting something at the crowd. A ragged dialogue followed. Tim couldn't catch any words, however. Finally the door closed behind the sheriff as the man moved off through the crowd.

The outer door opened a moment later. Above the crowd's noise, Tim heard the tramp of heavy boots as at least two men entered the sheriff's office. Tim sat down on the bunk and waited. The cell block door opened and Elias Bridger and Cass entered. Bridger carried a shotgun in the crook of his right arm and Cass was packing an enormous Colt in a worn leather holster. He strutted.

"The sheriff asked for deputies to help out," Bridger said. "I prevailed on Cass, here, to volunteer. He'll be out in the office, waiting for any fool to show his head."

Tim looked at the redhead. "Thanks, Cass."

"That's all right, Mr. Bolton."

"You just be sure," Tim said, smiling, "that you don't shoot your big toe off when you clear leather."

"I've been practicing," Cass said. He didn't smile at Tim's remark and was obviously a little upset at his kidding.

"I'm sure you have," said Tim.

"He'll be in the office if you need anything," said Bridger.

As Cass left the cell block ahead of Bridger, Tim called to the agent softly. Bridger pulled up and turned back to Tim's cell.

"What about you, Bridger? You going to be out there too?"

The man moistened his full lips. Tiny beads of perspiration stood out on his tall forehead. His white Stetson had been pushed back on his head. He was dressed almost funereally in a heavy dark suit. The shotgun he carried gleamed. "If the crowd gets any more unruly, I've told Cass to come get me."

"I see."

"I've wired San Francisco. They are leaving everything up to me. I think I'll offer Moses Kelly ten percent. Do you think he would accept that?"

"You'll have to ask him that, Bridger."

"Do you still have the money I gave you?"

Tim nodded.

"Good. Perhaps by morning this crowd will have tired itself out and you can still take that stage to Twin Forks."

"I hope so, Bridger."

"I'm . . . leaving now, Bolton."

"That's all right. I know I can count on you if things get any hotter. Thanks for putting yourself on the line like this."

The man appeared to flinch.

"Unlock this cell before you go, Bridger. I'm not going anywhere tonight. But if that crowd breaks in, I don't want to be trapped in here. Letting an Apache save your life isn't a crime yet, is it?"

The Wells, Fargo agent considered. Tim watched. At last Bridger took a deep breath. "The sheriff has the keys," he said. "They were in his hand when he accosted me outside."

"Why don't you see if you find the duplicates in his office?"

"I'll do that."

The man hurried from the cell block. Tim waited. After a hurried conversation with Cass, Bridger left the Sheriff's office. He had not even bothered to look for any duplicate set of keys. Tim had not really expected him to, however.

Tim went back to his bunk and lay down. He dozed.

Someone was haranguing the crowd. Tim sat up, suddenly alert. He recognized the voice. Slade Parkhurst. The gambler's words were punctuated by cries that swept the crowd. Parkhurst was carrying the crowd before him. They would soon bring swift and terrible justice to this man who counted the Apache among his friends.

"Cass!" Tim called, getting to his feet. Tim heard Cass stir. In a moment the young man was standing outside his cell door. He looked worried.

"Where's the sheriff, Cass?"

"He's trying to get more deputies, I guess. Said he was going to telegraph for the U.S. Deputy Marshall in Tularo."

"He won't get him in time, Cass. And he won't have any luck with deputies, either. You'll have to let me out of here."

"I couldn't. The sheriff didn't leave the keys."

"Shoot the lock out. I didn't commit any crime, Cass. Why should I be a prisoner in this jail?"

"But Mr. Bridger told me to keep you here so you won't get hurt."

"That crowd's going to be in here soon, Cass. And you'll be the first one they stomp over on their way in. Don't waste any more time. Shoot the lock off this cell door. And hurry it up."

Cass turned and looked toward the street. The crowd's roar was constant. Parkhurst's voice was quiet now, but another, heavier voice had taken over. Cass swallowed, took his enormous Colt out of his holster and stepped back. Tim went to the far corner of his cell. Cass gripped the revolver with both hands. He thumbcocked it and fired. The ancient lock exploded with the impact of the slug and the cell door hung slightly open.

Tim darted out of the cell and past Cass into the sheriff's office. The shot had carried to the crowd outside. Tim could hear that heavy voice again shouting something to the suddenly still crowd. Tim dug his six-gun out of a drawer in the sheriff's desk. then reached a Henry carbine down from the wall. It was fully loaded. He levered a cartridge into the firing chamber.

Glancing out the window, Tim saw a few torches lighting the night and casting a hellish glow over the crowd now surging in one solid mass toward the jail. Something heavy struck the door. A rock, perhaps.

Cass, standing beside Tim, glanced unhappily at Tim and swallowed. "They're gonna break down the door, Mr. Bolton."

What seemed like a pair of shoulders hit the door. Then a boot kicked at it. Tim stepped back into the cell block.

"Open the door, Cass," said Tim. "Tell them you're not going to try to stop them. Keep your hands up and they'll let you go."

"I can't do that, Mr. Bolton."

"Sure, you can. Do it, Cass, before it's too late."

"But . . . what about you?"

"Do it, Cass!"

Cass approached the door timidly. Again shoulders struck it from the other side, and this time the door splintered down the center, but held. Cass pulled open the door and two huge miners almost fell into the office.

Cass stepped back and flung up his hands. "Let me out," he cried. "I ain't gonna try and stop you! Let me out!"

The crowd roared and Tim heard some laughter. The two men grabbed Cass and flung him out past them into the night, then looked warily around the office. Both men had drawn their revolvers.

"Drop those guns," Tim said, stepping into full view in the cell block's doorway. "Then turn around."

When the two men hesitated, Tim raised the rifle to his shoulder. They dropped their weapons to the floor, then turned around. Three others were in the act of crowding into the jail after the men. When they saw them turning about with their hands in the air, they ducked back out of the office and plunged into the crowd, shouting out cries of warning.

"March!" said Tim.

The men walked out through the open door and Tim followed after them. He stopped in the open doorway and surveyed the crowd. It was large enough to completely fill the street from sidewalk to sidewalk and extended almost a block in either direction.

"Drop that gun, Apache lover!" someone in the back of the crowd yelled.

Tim lifted his rifle to his shoulder and fired over the top of the crowd in the direction from which the voice had come. He levered swiftly, went down on one knee, and squeezed off another shot, keeping his aim low enough so that those under the bullet's path could hear its passage. A window shattered as Tim's second round struck it.

The sound of the shattering windowpane seemed to galvanize the citizens. Where they had been frozen into immobility one moment, they scattered swiftly in both directions the next—like ants when a boot comes down on their nest.

A shot from Tim's left answered his shot, and a bullet ripped into the doorjamb over his head. Tim swung his rifle and squeezed off two quick shots in that direction, then darted into the night. People scattered in the darkness before him, their dim, faceless forms in a panic to get away. Some tripped and others fell over them. Tim, running now, had to jump to clear the huddled forms on the ground. A girl ducked away on his right. Swearing violently, she gathered up her skirt and raced like a man across the dark street.

Tim knew he could not keep exposing himself without taking a bullet. The crowd was pretty well dispersed by this time, isolating him in the street. As he ran down the street, the light from the saloons and the gas lamps fell upon him. Already he could see some men regrouping across the street.

A shot came from somewhere ahead of him. Splinters from a hitch rail he was passing flew up into his face. He ducked lower as a second shot, this one coming from across the street, sent a slug whining past his face and into a plate glass window that shivered and disintegrated. An alley opened on Tim's right. He darted into it.

At once the now thoroughly aroused citizens of Placerville streamed after him. There was not enough light in the alley for accurate firing, and it became a footrace. Tim was heading for the livery stable. It was a long chance, but he could see no other course of action but to hole up in the livery stable long enough to saddle his chestnut. Perhaps then he might be able to make a dash for it.

A horse appeared suddenly, galloping down the alley toward him. Tim heard shouts from others running down the alley toward him, men who had apparently almost been run down by the horse. There were loud, angry curses. A shot rang out. The horse and rider loomed over Tim with startling suddenness.

Tim ducked back against a flight of wooden stairs and raised the Henry.

"Up here!" the rider cried. "Swing up behind me!"

Instantly Tim recognized Bruder's voice—along with the heavy stench of raw whiskey. Tim dropped the rifle. Bruder's stocky figure leaned out of the saddle toward him. Tim grabbed the man's arm, kicked and swung up, then came down behind the cantle, his right arm firmly around Bruder's waist.

"Hang on!" Bruder cried as he dug his spurs into the horse's flank. "I ain't exactly sober yet!"

Tim did not reply. Once he got his left arm around Bruder's waist, he drew his six-gun. The men that had been pelting after Tim down the alley now flung themselves to one side as Bruder galloped through them. Once Bruder was past, they flung desperate shots after them. Tim did not bother to fire back.

And then they were out of the alley and turning down Main Street. A knot of men standing irresolutely in front of the Miner's Haven ran for their horses when they saw Bruder and Tim galloping toward them. Tim sent some bullets in their direction, however, and they scattered, diving into doorways and behind posts. A few shots followed them as they charged past the saloon. One bullet struck a street lamp. It winked out and Tim and Bruder galloped toward the jail under the cover of the sudden darkness.

As they passed the jail, Tim caught a glimpse of a dark figure standing in the shadow of the building, a rifle in his hand. It was raised. The barrel gleamed darkly, ominously, as it tracked them.

"Down," he told Bruder as he shifted his revolver to his left hand and tried to get off a shot.

The rifle cracked once, twice. Tim felt Bruder sag and heard the man's grunt. For a moment Tim thought Bruder was going to topple from his horse, but he pulled himself together and leaning well over the cantle spurred the horse out of town. As soon as they topped a rise and were well beyond the lights of the town, Bruder pulled up and released the reins.

Tim slid quickly to the ground and reached up to

help Bruder. The man's dead weight almost toppled Tim as he helped Bruder out of the saddle. He guided the man to a place under a cottonwood and helped him to a sitting position, his back propped up against the tree.

"I'm dead this time, Bolton," gasped Bruder.

In the darkness Tim could barely make out the man's face. He was speaking with his eyes closed, his mouth clamped tightly, his entire face twisted into a dark mask of pain. Without attempting to argue with the man, Tim looked for Bruder's wound.

Even in the profound darkness under the cottonwood Tim had little difficulty in finding it. There was a large hole in Bruder's left side, just under the rib cage. He quickly inspected the man's right side. There was no exit hole. He had not really expected any.

He swore softly.

"That's right, Bolton," Bruder gasped, "and that's just how it feels, too." He began to cough then, painfully, a congested sound to it.

"I'm sorry, Bruder," Tim said as he watched a thin dark line of blood tracing a path out of the left corner of Bruder's mouth. "You should have stayed out of this."

"Hell, you didn't stay out when I needed help, did you? You stuck your neck way out!" He spoke fiercely, with surprising animation. He reached out and grabbed Tim's arm. "Do you know why Parkhurst was trying to get me to draw on him?"

"No, Bruder. Why?"

"Because I knew about that gold shipment!" He coughed again. His hand gripped Tim's arm tighter, his fingers digging in like claws. "I knew all about it!" he gasped. "...knew what they was...planning!"

"Who, Bruder? Who's they?"

"Oh, Jesus!" the man gasped, twisting his head away from Tim, his eyeballs rolling up grotesquely. "That bullet! That damn bullet! Give me my six-gun, Bolton!"

"No, Bruder. Tell me. Who was in this with Parkhurst?"

Bruder looked at Tim. The pain in Bruder's eyes made Tim flinch. "I got you out of there, didn't I, Bolton?"

"Yes, you did, Bruder."

"I pay my debts, Bolton. I owed you—not them bastards! They kept my glass full all this time so I'd keep my mouth shut." He grinned then, though it was more like a grimace. "Only I crossed them when I saw you come back like that . . .!" Abruptly he gasped and swore, his eyes closing tightly.

When he opened them again, he was staring wildly past Tim as beads of sweat broke out suddenly all over his face. The pain was causing him to grimace continuously now. It was obvious to Tim that the wound was mortal. The trouble was it would take a while.

"It hurts, Bolton," the man whispered fiercely, his eyes focused with terrible intensity on Tim's face. "Give me that goddamn gun! Please, Bolton!"

Bruder slammed his head back against the tree suddenly and cried out—sounding like a wild, tongueless animal caught in some fearsome trap. Tim got to his feet, shaken. Deciding quickly, he bent, pulled Bruder's six-gun from the man's holster, and placed it carefully in his right hand.

Bruder opened his eyes. But he did not appear to see Tim. "Thanks, Bolton," he gasped. "Thanks for the gun. I really need this. It's . . . good for what ails me."

Tim straightened and looked down for a moment at the dying man. There was no sense in asking him any more questions. He had already told Tim enough, anyway.

"So long, Bruder," he said softly, aware that the man—wrapped in his cocoon of pain—could no longer see or hear him.

He turned and walked to Bruder's horse. He heard the six-gun thumbcocked as he swung into the saddle. He didn't look back. The shot came as he clapped his spurs to the dun and headed into the hills, on the other side of which he knew he would find the road leading to Twin Forks. He was not going to miss that meeting in the breaks with Bridger, after all.

Only Bridger didn't know that.

8

CAUGHT IN THE PITILESS glare of the mid-morning sun,
Amos Bruder's sprawled corpse had already attracted
a grim halo of buzzards wheeling above it in the sky. It
was this ominous sign that had drawn the posse. But
the impatient riders had no stomach for what they
would find and sat their horses, watching through the
cottonwoods as the sheriff and Slade Parkhurst stared
down at what was left of Amos Bruder.

"He must've bit right down on the barrel to lose the
back his head that way," said Turner, unable to keep
out of his voice a grudging note of respect.

Parkhurst turned and looked back through the trees
at the rest of the posse. It was obvious that his bullet
had led Bruder to this extremity. Yet, even though this
was not the first man he had killed, there was
something untidy, unsettling even, about the wide,
staring eyes, the torn skull. It was the awesomely
complete and utter lack of all life in what had once been
a sentient human being that was bothering him. For

the first time in his career Parkhurst was struck by the awful significance of what he had done.

Turner nudged him. "Neat, wouldn't you say? This settles it for Bolton."

Parkhurst turned back to the sheriff. At once he saw what Turner was driving at. In that moment he dismissed completely any qualms he had been feeling. He smiled quickly, his eyes remaining icy. "Yes. Poor Bruder," he said. "Killed by the very man he had helped to escape. A nice ironical twist, I must admit."

Turner contemplated Bruder with some satisfaction. Then he leaned over and with quick, tough motions freed the gun from Bruder's cold grasp. Tossing the six-gun ten feet or more from the body, he tucked the toe of his boot under Bruder's shoulder and kicked the stiffening body over onto its face. The gaping skull caused Turner to look away.

"Let me do the talking," he told the gambler as he led Parkhurst back through the trees to the waiting posse.

"It's Bruder, Forrest," the sheriff told the first rider he approached. "Looks like him and Bolton had a falling out. Bolton shot him twice. Once in the back of the head. Not very pretty."

Forrest shook his head. He was the town's sole pharmacist, a tall, thin, cadaverous fellow of thirty-five. "Sonofabitch, Sheriff. That sure as hell don't sound so good, does it." Forrest's horse seemed as unnerved as its rider was by this announcement. The animal shook his head vigorously and snorted. Forrest gentled the animal with a reassuring pat on its neck. "What are we going to do now?"

"Bury the sonofabitch, I reckon," said Turner.

He looked past the pharmacist to the rest of the

posse still bunched outside the cottonwoods. "Hey, Grunewald!" he called to one of the riders. "You want to haul Bruder's body back into town and bury it?"

Grunewald was the town's only undertaker. He was a broad, bloated rider that appeared to ooze out over his saddle. He took off his wide, floppy-brimmed hat and mopped his forehead with a red bandanna. "Bruder?"

"You heard me."

"Who's paying for the burial?" Grunewald wanted to know, the effort to talk causing him to wheeze. "The town?"

"The town, hell."

Grunewald and the rest of the riders kneed their horses closer until they had formed a semicircle around the sheriff and Slade. The sheriff looked up at the tired faces.

"Then we give Amos to the buzzards," he told them.

A few riders frowned at the callousness of this suggestion, but most kept their faces impassive. There was no spoken dissent.

"Okay, then. We'll let the birds have him and get on after Bolton."

Forrest cleared his throat nervously. "Sheriff, I really can't stay with this posse any longer. I have a business to take care of. Besides, it looks to me like Bolton's already safe with his Apache friends."

"Suit yourself," said Turner. "Go on back if you want." The sheriff's glance raked the rest of the faces staring glumly down at him. "What about the rest of you? You want to cut out, too?"

The men nodded heavily, every one of them. They had had it. The sun was lifting higher in the gleaming sky. Their wives and their work were well behind them in Placerville. Hours of riding over this treacherous ground had left them muscle-racked, raw with saddle gall.

Grunewald, still mopping his forehead hopelessly, said, "I guess we'll all be riding back, Sheriff."

"What about you, Sheriff?" asked Burt Standish. He was the town's blacksmith, a powerful fellow with hair and brows and eyes as black and shiny as newly mined coal.

"I'm staying on Bolton's trail. So's Slade."

"That means you'll be leaving town without any law."

"I can't help it. This guy Bolton is a murderer now. I've got to bring him in and that's a fact." Turner paused then and looked shrewdly at the blacksmith. "You want me to deputize you in my absence?"

The fellow's eyes gleamed darkly. It was what he wanted, all right. It was why he had reminded Turner that he was leaving Placerville without law. "All right, Sheriff. That suits me."

"All right then. You'll be acting sheriff. I'll give you power to deputize anyone else you need."

The sheriff looked around at the others.

"Any of you men not willing I should leave Burt in charge?"

Not a head moved. A few looked at the blacksmith appraisingly. They knew and respected the man. He would do, they figured.

"It's settled then. Ride on back to town. Slade and I will follow Bolton's trail as far as we can."

"Watch out for them Apaches, Sheriff," Burt Standish called, as he spun his horse about and charged back through the posse.

Turner just waved and watched as the riders quickly strung out behind the eager blacksmith. When the dust had settled, he looked with gleaming eyes at Slade. Abruptly, he broke into laughter and slapped Parkhurst resoundingly on the back.

They had done it—shaken the posse without arousing suspicion. Now they were free to continue on alone after Bolton. They knew that when they found Bolton, they would also find Bridger and that prospector, Moses.

And the gold.

Ahead of Tim the hills sloped off rapidly toward the badlands. It lay now like a molten red tangle of peaks and buttes in the last glow of the sinking sun. The old cattleman's trail he was following was splitting up as its broad trace flowed around outcroppings of rock and stands of pine or clumps of aspen.

His mount settled into a punishing downhill lope as the trail dropped into another steep canyon. At the sight of water rushing white across a rocky ford, Tim pulled up to let his horse blow and drink. He eased himself out of the saddle and filled his canteen, looking about cautiously as he did so.

He was now between Twin Forks and the badlands and would soon reach the road the stage had used on its way into the badlands. Once out of the breaks and as soon as he reached the road, he would select a suitable spot and wait for Bridger to show. Tim had ridden straight across the hills without cutting south into Twin Forks. There was little doubt in his mind but that Bridger—having had to spend time in Twin Forks to purchase four pack mules and supplies—was still behind him.

But not too far, perhaps.

The only question remaining was, would Bridger take this road? Having considered the alternatives carefully, Tim saw no reason for Bridger not to take it. Any other route into the badlands would only invite needless aggravation in addition to delaying him. Yes, Bridger would take the stage road—and he would be alone. The sheriff could not leave Placerville. Parkhurst had obviously stayed behind to stir up the crowd. It was he who had shot at them as they rode past the jail. The blood of Amos Bruder was again on Parkhurst's hands—only this time it was for keeps.

Turner and Parkhurst were in this with Bridger, of course, but the agent was too shrewd—too careful—a man to let those two accompany him into the badlands after that gold.

Tim mounted up and rode on back to the trail and put his horse on down the steep slope. The crimson earth was slashed by winding, sheer-walled draws, deceptive and deadly as pitfalls; but the cattleman's trail kept through the breaks, finding always the natural, the safest way to the valley floor below. At last Tim saw the raw, almost chalk-white scar that was the stagecoach route to California. It cut from behind a towering butte to Tim's left and disappeared into the badlands directly ahead.

Between the road and Tim there was a river. Tim rode out of the last of the pine and aspen, cut through the sage and juniper. The river was high and fast, but he found a ford. The water tugged at the horse's belly, but the horse found the opposite bank without much trouble. Tim led the horse for a while to save it and soon found himself beside the road. Looking back along it, he saw no cover.

Ahead, however, he saw where the road crowded between two low buttes. He mounted up and rode toward them. The closer he got, the more he liked them. It was almost dark when he reached the small tableland atop the lowest butte. Below him, less than twenty feet, the surface of the road gleamed in the swiftly-gathering darkness. He would camp here and wait until Bridger passed—or until he was certain Bridger was not coming this way.

Bridger had long since crossed his Rubicon when he conspired with Bart Talbot. It was an insignificant step further into damnation for him to have allowed the sheriff and Parkhurst to become a part of his plans now. And when he had the gold finally, he would kill them all, every man jack of them and live in the splendor such wealth would provide.

As he rode now through the gathering darkness, his mind—filled with the darker shadows of his past—ran along ahead of him in a fever of anticipation. What he anticipated was hell on the one hand, and hell on the other. That was the rub. He was already a doomed soul. He could hear, even now, above the patient clop of the four mules and his own mount, the screams of his soul as it twisted in torment throughout all eternity.

He had come west thirteen years before, a married minister of the Calvinist persuasion. In his arrogance and pride he had sought out the rowdiest, most Godforsaken sink of iniquity in which to begin his ministry, the aptly-named Devil's Gap, a mining center of fourteen thousand souls, all rushing at a breakneck pace to perdition with the aid of thirty-five brothels, one-hundred-and-eighteen gambling dens, and one-hundred-and-twenty saloons. As he had complained one day to his wife, he would never know when Sunday came around if he didn't keep track of the days religiously. His church was an abandoned feed mill on the outskirts of town and so empty of parishoners that, in desperation, he attempted to bring his ministry to the afflicted souls who dwelt in the infamous red-light district.

His efforts brought only hoots of derision at first, and when he persisted, worse. He had full jugs of night soil emptied on him. Whiskey was forcibly poured down his protesting throat. More than once he had ridden home without his trousers. Yet nothing could discourage him. He returned each day with renewed enthusiasm—never questioning the attraction the saloons and brothels held for him. So innocent was he, after all, of the workings of that dark master, Satan.

At last he tasted success—or what he thought was success—when what was the most infamous and wealthy madam in the town confessed to him that she wished to follow Jesus. He ministered to her for a full week. He prayed with her, ate with her, kept himself on hand to be at her side whenever she weakened. And Oh, the tales she told! The lurid accounts of her incredible licentiousness!

On the sixth night, while he slept fitfully, she had come to his bed craving a boon—a small favor, as she put it. The weakness of her flesh threatened to overwhelm her. Perhaps he could see it in his heart to minister to her body as well as her soul. . . .

He never returned to the feed mill—or his wife. And only gradually was he able to construct another mask to cover the blasted wasteland that was his soul. His education soon came to his aid and he found employment at first as a newspaperman and then as an agent with Wells, Fargo.

But the devil had him in his palm now and there was no sense in denying his awesome power. If Elias was to be damned for all eternity for his transgressions on this earth, he had best make the most of what time he had left. And that is what he was doing at the moment, he reminded himself, as he urged his horse on through the darkness.

The moon climbed into the sky, its great baleful cat's eye burning down on him, sending its silver sheen ahead of him along the road. It was Satan's eye, of course, sending this aid to help one of his own. What was it they called the badlands? The Devil's Playground. Elias chuckled and looked appreciatively up at the moon, blazing now in the night sky.

Abruptly the moon vanished behind one of the two buttes that flanked the road ahead. As he rode into the inky blackness between the two towering rock masses, a voice called softly to him from above.

For just the tiniest second Bridger's heart stopped. Satan was addressing one of his children! He shook himself angrily at the thought. Again the voice, louder this time, called out to him.

"Bridger!"

Elias pulled up, furious. He recognized the voice. It was that of Tim Bolton! How had that man escaped the sheriff?

He patted the horse's neck, inwardly seething. In a few moments he heard someone drop lightly to the ground just ahead of him. Then, out of the gloom, strode Bolton.

"I see you got the pack mules, all right," Bolton said. Elias wasn't sure, but he thought he saw a smile on the man's face.

"Yes," Bridger replied. "I . . . didn't think you'd be able to get them in time."

"I got lucky again. I busted out of the jail. So here I am. Why don't you camp here for the night? I got a good spot up here on the butte."

"Sounds like a fine idea. I'm quite worn out."

Bridger was confused. How much, he wondered, did Bolton suspect, if anything. Bolton took hold of his mount's bridle and turned the animal about until Bridger was riding back the way he had come. The mules followed along docilely and soon they were climbing to the top of the butte. The embers of a campfire lit their way to Bolton's camp.

Bridger dismounted, surprised at how stiff he had become. He squinted through the darkness at Bolton, trying to discern some motive in the man's face. But the fellow seemed entirely devoid of any suspicion, almost cheerful. At the moment he was with the mules, seeing to their hobbles and sizing them up. Next he inspected the *aparejos*.

Bridger walked over to the still warm embers and held his hands out over them. The desert chill only now seemed to be reaching into his bones. Glancing over at Bolton, he wondered what the fellow could possibly see in the dark. Bolton looked over at him, then came toward him.

"That's leather, padded leather on those *aparejos*," he said, coming to a halt across the campfire from Bridger. "You don't want to take a chance on losing any of that gold, do you."

He knows, Bridger thought, almost with relief.

"Penny wise and pound foolish if I bought cheap canvas ones. I did not have much choice in Twin Forks."

"The mules look strong enough."

"They cost an arm and a leg."

"Well, as you say. It's a good investment."

"How... did you manage to get out of that jail so quickly? From the looks of that mob, I didn't see much hope in your leaving its protection at least until morning."

"Cass let me out last night and Amos Bruder came by with a horse. Parkhurst shot and killed Bruder as we rode out. The sheriff made himself scarce." Bolton smiled, his teeth gleaming in the moonlight. "If I had stayed in that jail I wouldn't have been able to meet you—like we planned."

"Well...I am certainly surprised—and delighted, of course—that you got away."

"Of course you are."

Bridger took a deep breath. "Why don't we dispense with this sparring, Bolton? We both know that I had no intention of meeting you in the breaks—that I had intended to go ahead of you to Kelly's cabin, and from there to Diablo Canyon. You see, I didn't really need you, once the sheriff told me how to reach this prospector's cabin."

"So you told the sheriff."

"I felt I had to."

"And he told Slade Parkhurst."

"I imagine he did. I promised the sheriff a portion of the gold when I return. If he wants to share it with Parkhurst, that's his business."

"And what about me?"

"I'm prepared to grant you a share, of course."

"Now that I've turned up again—like a bad penny."

"Yes."

"How much, Bridger?"

"A generous amount, I assure you."

"What are your assurances worth, Bridger? You set me up nicely with that note suggesting that I ride out last night. You had the sheriff waiting for me in the stable so he could shanghai me into that jail. Parkhurst and the mob would do the rest. Or so you figured."

"I was wrong, obviously."

"Besides, Bridger. That gold's not yours to parcel

out to others. It belongs to Wells, Fargo. Or had you forgotten?"

"Don't be a fool, Bolton! It belongs to us—once we find it."

"You tipped Bart Talbot when to expect the gold shipment."

Bridger did not feel he needed to admit that. It was obvious, and he felt uncomfortable agreeing with Bolton. Indeed, the man's quiet, seething disapproval was most disconcerting. Damn him! He reminded Elias of a much younger, even more idealistic youth. . . .

"You're right, Bridger. You don't have to bother to admit that. But tell me, why did the sheriff pour that whiskey drummer onto the stage along with all that gold?"

"The drummer held more then a thousand of Turner's IOUs. Slade's as well. Despite his love for the brew he sold, he was a fine poker player, it seems."

"The three of us were expendable then. The whiskey drummer, me, Charlie West. It was Slade's idea that you give me the job riding shotgun, wasn't it."

Bridger nodded.

"Lovely. The three of you make quite a team."

"Throw in with us, Bolton. There's enough gold for all of us."

"I guess I'll just have to trust you to keep your part of the bargain. Is that it?"

"Just as I will have to trust you."

"We'll both have to be very careful then, won't we. Turn around, Bridger."

"Why?"

"Just do it." As he spoke Bridger saw the six-gun appear in Bolton's right hand.

Bridger turned his back on Bolton. He heard the

man walk around the campfire. There was a pause. Bridger started to turn and felt the sky drop onto his head. He was unconscious before he struck the ground.

Tim was careful to see that Bridger did not fall into the still-glowing embers of the campfire. Then he searched the man thoroughly, relieving him of a small derringer as well as his holstered Smith & Wesson. Afterwards he dragged him over to one of the mules, threw him across the padded *aparejos*, trussed him securely, then kicked out the campfire and rolled into his soogan.

He did not sleep at once.

His anger at this man whom he now realized was the author of so much misery had not been appeased by the violent manner in which he had just put him to sleep, though it had helped some. He would not be content until he saw Bridger behind bars—along with the sheriff and Parkhurst—and the gold back in the coffers of Wells, Fargo. With these pack mules and the provisions so thoughtfully provided by Bridger, he and Moses Kelly would have a much easier time retrieving the gold.

Tim's motive was not entirely altruistic. Wells, Fargo was just a name to him, but he knew there would be a substantial reward from the company—and that Moses Kelly would get a generous portion of it. Tim wanted him to have the money—for himself as well as for Marylou.

As Tim closed his eyes at last and drifted off to sleep, his inner eye saw Marylou as he remembered her when he rode away from the miner's cabin a few days ago and saw again the fearful, tentative smile she had dared send his way.

Tim slept.

9

IT WAS MARYLOU TIM saw first a little past noon as he broke out of the canyon and started across the flat to the miner's cabin. She watched him approach for a second or two, as still and as startled as a wild animal. Then she broke for the cabin.

Moses Kelly appeared in the doorway before Marylou reached the place. He caught her up in his arms and appeared to shake some sense into her. Then he let her go. She vanished inside the cabin.

Moses waved to him and called out. Tim was too dry to answer his call. He just waved. Behind him Bridger's groan broke the stillness of the torrid wasteland. Tim did not even bother to look back at the man.

"Who the hell you got there?" Moses demanded when Tim drew close enough for the man to see the burden one of the mules was carrying.

"I'll explain later."

The miner stroked his long white beard reflectively as he watched the tall agent in his heavy dark suit suffering through the rigors of his ride. Slung like a sack over the mule's back, Bridger seemed intent only on groaning feebly. There was, Tim detected, a sudden twinkle in the old prospector's eyes when he recognized the Wells, Fargo agent.

"That's Bridger, ain't it," Moses said, glancing happily at Tim.

Tim nodded.

"That's a hell of a way to transport the fellow who's about to see us get a fat reward for helping him get back all that Wells, Fargo gold."

Tim dismounted. "Hell, Moses, this sonofabitch engineered that raise with Bart Talbot and his men. That's how come they knew which stage to raise in the first place and where the gold was hidden inside the stage. I watched them. They went right to work ripping up the floorboards as soon as the stage came to rest."

"Well, well," said Moses as he stepped back a ways to get a better view of Bridger's beet-red face. The man was trying to twist his face around to see where he was. "I should have figured it, Tim. I never liked the man. Too much of an education. Carried himself around like he was something special, like he maybe didn't use toilet paper the way the rest of us had to."

Tim smiled and untied Bridger's wrists and ankles. The man's wrists were bloody where the rawhide had cut into the flesh. Bridger slid to the ground and curled up like a huge rag doll.

"Give me a hand," the man mumbled through cracked lips.

Tim and Moses reached down, caught the man under his arms, and lifted him to his feet. With a half-hearted gesture of defiance the tall fellow tried to push away from them and take a step on his own. He succeeded only in buckling at the knees. Tim and

Moses caught him and dragged him upright, then steered him into the cabin.

They gave him a seat at the table. The man leaned forward onto it to regain his equilibrium, then glared around at the two men. "Give me something to drink, damn you!" he whispered hoarsely.

Moses glanced over at Marylou, who was standing by the sink. She quickly dipped a tin cup into a bucket of spring water sitting on the drain board and brought the dripping cup over to Bridger. The man snatched it from her and drank it greedily.

"More," he told her, handing the cup back.

"You'll get sick," cautioned Moses.

"Damn both of you to hell! What do you care if I get sick or not?"

"It'll make a mess on the floor," said Tim.

Bridger flung himself back in the chair, his blazing, furious glance moving from one to the other. "Just what are your intentions concerning me?"

"We'll leave you here and go after the gold," Tim said. "Then we'll bring it and you in."

"To Placerville?"

"That's right."

"The townsmen will tear you limb from limb." He glanced at Moses. "Both of you Apache lovers."

Tim smiled. "I figured I'd telegraph Wells, Fargo in San Francisco from Twin Forks first. Sort of make sure of my welcome."

The fire in the man's eyes died. He looked down at the table in front of him, then ran his long fingers through his hair. "Let me go, Bolton," he said. "What's it to you if I go free or not?"

"I'll see you hung, Bridger—and enjoy every minute of it. I liked Charlie West—and Amos Bruder saved my life."

"It's vengeance you want, is it?"

"Justice, Bridger."

"You haven't got the gold yet, I notice. And I'm a long way from a hangman's noose at this moment."

Tim glanced at Moses Kelly. "He's right. We haven't got that gold yet. Any sign of Naretena and his Apaches?"

Moses smiled. "I told you. He's gone to Victorio. I gave his last two bucks brand new Winchesters when they brought you in. They'll be showing off their new weapons to Victorio. They might just break them in with a raid on some Mex Rancho."

"But they'll be back. For more carbines."

"Diablo Canyon's a four-five-hour ride. We could reach it by nightfall if we left now."

"I think we should then."

Moses nodded. He turned to Marylou. "Fill our canteens at the spring," he told her. "All of them."

She went to one of the trunks and took out four army canteens. As she went to the door with them, Tim spoke up. "Wait a minute, Marylou. I've got a canteen I want filled too." She stopped and looked at him. "So maybe I'll go with you, give you a hand."

Fear crossed her face with the speed of a summer cloud, then vanished. She glanced once at Moses, then looked back at Tim. What was almost a smile brightened her face as she nodded quickly, then turned and darted out of the door.

He caught up to her a few moments later bent over a rocky ledge, dipping one of the canteens into the reddish stream that flowed out of a crack in the cliff face that leaned crookedly over them. The shade cooled him at once and the sound of the running water was like music to his soul after the unrelenting heat of the flat. He got down on one knee beside her and unscrewed the cap to his canteen, glancing at her as he did so.

She caught his glance. He thought he saw her face color. And she did not flinch away. He dipped the canteen into the stream, letting the icy water coil about his wrist. It sent delicious tentacles of coolness sweeping up his arm. He withdrew the suddenly heavy canteen and reached for the cap. As he screwed it on he looked at Marylou again, this time studying her more closely.

It seemed to him that there was much less of that gaunt angularity about her face. She had filled out some. She was burned brown now and her light hair was bleached to the color of corn silk. Out of her brown face, her blue eyes stared at him like patches of blue sky through storm clouds. The pinched lips and the grim line of her mouth had softened. She no longer gave Tim the impression of a captured bird. And yet there remained a fragile wildness about her that cautioned him.

She trusted him, he knew. Even so, any overt act on his part, any hasty attempt on his part to draw too close would startle her back into herself—like a deer bounding back into the timber.

"Let me carry some of those canteens back to the cabin for you," he said.

She nodded and handed him one. "Thank you," she said.

Tim was startled by the clear sound of her voice. This was the first time he had heard it. She uttered the two words shakily, the way it is after a long illness when you're not quite sure the vocal chords are still functioning.

"That's all right," he replied hastily, almost dropping the canteen she was handing to him.

He looked quickly at her and saw the ghost of a smile on her face.

"Only I'm not looking forward to that walk across the flat," Tim went on quickly, eager now to make conversation. He felt deeply moved, humbled even, by this breakthrough—this obvious sign of her trust—and he did not want to let this opportunity pass without making the most of it.

"It *is* very hot," she agreed shyly. "I use Moses's hat usually. But it is so big I have to hold it on." She sat back then and looked at him. "I am not afraid of you, Tim. I thought of you while you were gone. I am glad you have come back. But I do not like this other one." Her face clouded. "I am afraid he will bring trouble for you and Moses."

She laughed suddenly, then caught herself by clapping one hand over her mouth.

"What's the matter?" Tim asked, alarmed.

"It is me," she replied in wonder. "All of a sudden I talk too much." She frowned then and reached out to touch his arm. The touch was shy. Tim could barely feel its weight. "It is like a part of me has come out of darkness." She looked at Tim with wonder. "It has been so long," she said, her voice suddenly hushed.

"I'm glad," he told her.

"I am glad, too. But . . . I am afraid." She closed her eyes, let go of his arm, and sat back suddenly. "So much has happened . . . !"

"It's going to be all right now."

She opened her eyes and looked at him. The trust in them was almost more than Tim could bear. "Yes," she said softly. "Yes, Tim."

The sunlight had reached them while they talked. Now, as Marylou spoke, two hulking shadows fell over them. Turning, Tim started to get to his feet. A gun

butt crashed down onto the back of his skull and he
pitched forward into darkness.

Slade smiled at Turner.

"Thanks," he said, holstering his gun and looking
back down at the sprawled figure of Tim Bolton. "I
been wanting to do that for some time .ow."

Slade looked at the girl. Nice, he thoug it. Very nice.
A true desert flower, something to keep away the desert
chill. That old goat Moses Kelly should be ashamed of
himself.

"Don't get upset, girl," he said to her. "We won't
hurt you. Not if you play nice—like you were playing
just now with Bolton."

The expression on the girl's face did not change with
Slade's words, however. The look on her face annoyed
Slade. She just stared at him, eyes wide, face frozen
into a mask of horror. Slade took a step toward her,
reached down, and snatched at her wrist. Pulling her to
her feet, he flung an arm around her neck, grabbed a
fistful of her golden hair, and pulled her head back so
that she was looking up into his face.

He bent his face to hers then, intending to force a
kiss. But an ugly, startling transformation came over
the girl's face. It became pinched, the eyes narrowing,
the lines about the mouth thin and cold. It was as if a
light within her had suddenly been blown out. He flung
her to the ground.

She landed on her hands and knees like a wild thing,
her head twisted down and away from him.

"The hell with you," Slade told her.

Turner laughed. "You discourage easy."

"I do not need to force myself on a woman, Turner,"
Slade said to the sheriff, bending now to remove
Bolton's six-gun from its holster. "I am not like those

filthy animals who keep the cribs in back of the Miner's Haven so busy."

"Hell, you ain't," said Turner, shaking his head at the gambler's peculiar airs.

Slade shrugged. It was not a bone of contention between them. Slade did not begrudge the sheriff his impatience with Slade's more constrained, southern view of things. There was no way, Slade was convinced, that you could teach a Yankee what it meant to be a gentleman. The entire concept was beyond a Yankee's feeble understanding.

Slade saw Bolton stir. The man's hand went to the back of his head. He groaned and sat up suddenly, squinting through painful eyes up at the two of them.

Turner smiled at him. "Now we got you, Bolton. For the murder of poor Amos Bruder. We found him where you left him. We've been on your trail ever since."

"But before we bring you in for that despicable crime," Slade said, ".we shall see to that gold. Get up. You will precede us, sir, to the old man's cabin."

As Bolton got slowly to his feet, Turner chuckled. "We watched the way you handled Bridger. He sure as hell is going to like the way we turned the tables for him, don't you think?"

Bolton appeared to be having trouble keeping his knees under him. Slade grabbed his left shoulder and spun him around. Then he placed his boot against the Texan's backside and gave him a powerful shove in the direction of the cabin. The big man stumbled, but managed to keep his feet.

"Don't say nothin' alarming," the sheriff cautioned Bolton, "or we'll kill you—and the girl."

"That's right," Slade said. "You won't be giving us

any choice then." As Slade spoke he reached down and pulled the girl to her feet and shoved her after Bolton.

She kept up with Bolton in a kind of crouch, looking for all the world like something half-wild. Abruptly she broke into a run and fled ahead of them with surprising swiftness across the rocky ground.

"Don't shoot her," Bolton told him, stopping and turning to face him.

"No, I won't shoot her," Slade replied. "But I will you if you don't keep going."

Bolton turned back around and the two men followed him across the flat. When they were about halfway, Moses Kelly appeared in the doorway. Slade recognized him from the times this past summer when he visited the Miner's Haven. He had seemed surprisingly flush, yet he had never tarried for long and never gambled. Each time, however, he bought a round for the place just before he shoved off again. The girl was behind Moses, peering out at them over his shoulder.

Slade said nothing to Moses. Neither did the sheriff. They just kept going. Not until they were a few yards from the miner's cabin did Slade draw his revolver and tuck its muzzle into Bolton's back. As he did so, he smiled at Moses Kelly.

"Did you know you were harboring a criminal, Moses?" the gambler asked. "Yessir. This here no-account Texan murdered Amos Bruder."

"No, he didn't."

"Yes, he did," said the sheriff.

They were at the cabin doorway by then. Moses hesitated, then stepped back into the cabin. Slade rammed the muzzle of his revolver deep into Bolton's back. The fellow lurched ahead of him through the doorway, caught himself at the table, and hung on to it.

It was surprisingly cool inside the miner's cabin and Slade felt almost immediate relief from the crushing weight of the heat outside. He holstered his gun and looked around for Bridger.

The tall agent was standing beside the door, a look of pure, undiluted pleasure on his long, gaunt face. His large dark eyes, usually brooding, were alight now with triumph. Turner had hit the nail square on the head back there. The agent was pleased as hell at this abrupt reversal of his fortune.

"Where the hell did you two drop from?" Bridger asked, his voice powerful with relief and pleasure at his deliverance.

"Never mind that," said Turner. "You got the mules, so let's get after that gold. Now."

Bridger frowned. "Wait just a minute. I've had quite an experience, a somewhat grueling experience, I might add. I doubt if I can ride so soon."

"I know, I know," snapped Turner. "Slade and I watched the whole thing. Bolton here wasn't very gentle at that. What do you want us to do with him?"

"We don't need him," Bridger replied, turning to regard Bolton with malicious pleasure.

Slade stood back and watched, amused. He didn't know where Bridger came from, but he was a tricky customer. Sometimes he acted like a preacher, other times like the devil himself. At the moment the devil in the man was in full control.

"That so?" Turner said, glancing idly at Bolton.

"As soon as I heard that Moses Kelly here knew where the canyon was, I realized that was all I needed. Bart told me he had found a mine shaft in a canyon where he would stash the gold. Of course he didn't tell me where the canyon was. That's up to Moses now. But there can't be more than one or two mine shafts in that canyon."

"So we don't need Bolton to show us where the mine shaft is, then?" Slade asked, moving closer now and enjoying the look on Bolton's face.

"No," Bridger said emphatically. "We don't need him at all."

"Wait a minute," said Moses. "Who says I'm takin' you animals to that canyon?"

Slade was surprised at the old man's truculence. He smiled at him and said, "We do. You're taking us to that canyon, old man."

"No, I'm not."

Moses was less than a couple of feet from Slade. Slade slapped Moses as hard as he could. The old man was knocked back a few steps by the force of the blow.

Slade looked beyond Moses to the girl cringing by the sink. "If slapping you don't help, old man, I'll start on that girl back there. Looks to me like she needs someone to take her in hand."

"Is that what your fine southern manners amounts to?" Bolton inquired, his voice low, dangerous.

Slade turned to him. "Southern manners for southern *ladies*, Bolton. And if I were you, I wouldn't speak until I was spoken to."

"Touch her and you'll answer to me."

Slade smiled. "That so? Why, sir, you tempt me."

"All right," said Moses, glowering at Slade. "But we need Bolton. He goes too."

"Why?" asked the sheriff.

"There's a helluva lot more than one mine shaft in that canyon. I ought to know. I dug most of them these past ten years. And that ain't just one canyon. Not really. Once you get in there, it's like a maze, smaller canyons shooting off in all directions, if you know what I mean."

"We know what you mean," said Bridger, obviously offended that Moses should doubt his ability to understand him. "You mean Bolton knows which mine shaft?"

Moses shrugged. Then he looked at Bolton. "He watched them stash it, then waited for them to make camp before he made his move."

Slade moved swiftly, grabbed Moses's left arm and spun him around. "Damn you, old man! You're putting words into Bolton's mouth!"

Moses braced himself defiantly, ready for whatever Slade might do next. Furious, Slade glanced over at Bolton.

"I suppose you're going to agree with the old bastard."

The tall man shrugged, the ghost of a smile on his face. "He was just telling it the way it was. If you want to know which mine shaft, you'll have to take me with you."

Slade looked at the sheriff. "Take him." Then he looked around at Moses and Bolton. "But I promise you, gentlemen. We'll find the correct mine shaft. One way or the other, we'll find it. Or your bones will whiten in the noon sun before this week is out."

"What about the girl?" Turner asked.

"Take her too," Slade answered quickly. "I'll find a use for her. She can ride up behind Bolton. These desert nights get pretty chilly. And I like a little exercise before I bed down."

Slade caught the look in Bolton's eyes and laughed in his face at his reaction. He found that he was enjoying himself, tingling all over with the excitement of it. It was a pleasure to get away from the gaming table once in a while, especially when the stakes were this high.

Turner was looking at Bridger. "You ready to ride, Bridger? We don't really need you either, you know." The sheriff spoke with the trace of a smile on his face, but there was a cold watchfulness in Turner's eyes, which told the agent that the sheriff was not entirely jesting.

Bridger looked from the sheriff to Parkhurst, measuring their resolve carefully. His long, sensuous face hardened with resolve. "Of course I'm ready," he said.

In less than an hour they were heading for Diablo Canyon, strung out across the tortuous rocky fastness of the Devil's Playground. Moses Kelly, the sheriff, and Bridger rode in the lead. Behind them came Bolton with the girl they called Marylou. Both were leading the mules. Parkhurst rode on the right swing, far enough out to keep free of the dust being raised, yet close enough for him to be able to keep a sharp eye on Bolton and the girl.

Moses, Slade figured, was old enough not to care all that much about himself and would have to be watched carefully. The girl was obviously his pet—and that meant they could keep Moses in line simply by threatening the girl. Tim Bolton was a different matter. He was dangerous, very dangerous.

The man walked tall and did not hesitate when he knew he was right. He had pride and a controlled fury that made him contemptuous of all those whose weaknesses made them less than he. Something fierce burned within him—burned with an intensity that shone in everything he said, every action he took. The problem was he was honest. No one, Slade observed ironically to himself, is more frightening, more impossible to deal with than a person you cannot corrupt, one who is immune to all temptation. That was what made Bolton so dangerous.

This was why Slade hated the Texan with a fury so corrosive he found it difficult to keep under rein. Slade recognized in Bolton those qualities he would have liked—at one time—to have possessed himself. The truth was that the Texan reminded him of all that he might have been.

Slade nudged his horse closer. Bolton rode tall in the saddle, easy for his own comfort and even-balanced to save the horse, since it must carry the girl as well. His lean, flat-planed face showed no emotion, but his eyes were alert and three-quarters lidded to shield them from the glare. There was nothing soft about the man, not a spare ounce of flesh on his lean frame. Though Slade had not held back when he brought his gun butt down on his skull earlier, the man looked as fresh and as alert as any of them, despite the almost withering heat.

Without warning, Bolton turned his head and looked straight at Slade, his eyes regarding the gambler coolly from under the brim of his black Plains hat—*Clint Andersen's hat,* Parkhurst realized suddenly.

Slade returned the Texan's stare, fighting to control the knife-edge of fear those eyes of Bolton's planted in his gut. Those eyes and the sight of Clint's hat. Bolton had taken that from Clint, and Clint had been the best of the lot. Slade had liked Clint. The man played a good hand and never complained when he lost—even when he knew why he lost.

Bolton looked back at the trail ahead.

Slade turned his attention then to the girl. She rode behind Bolton with one hand around his waist, the other gripping the mules' lead. How the hell had the old reprobate latched onto a filly like that in the middle of this wasteland? She was obviously a mite shy, frightened even. But that was not altogether displeasing—especially after the whores he had had to content himself with lately. A girl who was fresh and shy for a change would be a delight.

Slade nudged his horse and guided it farther to his right, away from the dust the four horses and the mules were raising. When he looked back again, he fixed his attention on the Texan.

He was too dangerous to live. Slade was angry with himself for not killing Bolton when he came upon him with the girl. Well, he would take the first opportunity to rid himself of the man. He did not believe they needed the Texan to find that mine shaft.

To let him live any longer than was necessary was only asking for trouble. Once he had settled this in his mind, Slade relaxed and felt better. After all, he reminded himself complacently, when you have all the high cards, that's the time to make your play.

They had been riding over what seemed like impossible terrain for close to three hours when Moses turned in his saddle and beckoned toward a water hole well off the trail they were following. Slade had some water left in his canteen only because he had been husbanding it in a miserly fashion and was glad of the opportunity this gave him to fill his canteen and drink deeply for the first time in a long while.

Slade was the last to reach the water hole. It was not a pleasant-looking pool, quite scummy, the water red-tinged. But it would have to do. The sheriff and

Bridger were getting ready to dip their canteens into
the water. As Slade went down on one knee and
unscrewed the cap to his own canteen, the girl—
evidently very thirsty—went down on both knees
beside Bridger and leaning over formed a cup with
both her hands and dipped it into the pool.

As she was carrying the water to her lips, however,
Moses deliberately bumped her. The girl's hands
opened as she caught herself, the water spilling away.
Slade had seen the action clearly. Moses did not want
the girl to drink from this water hole.

"Hold it, Bridger—Sheriff!" Slade called out
sharply, getting swiftly to his feet. "Don't drink any of
this water! It's poisoned!"

Both men turned to look at him in astonishment.
Slade whipped out his six-gun and brought the barrel
down with vicious force on the side of Moses's head.
The old man gasped and fell sideways, a bright red
stain rapidly issuing from the gash that had been
opened just behind his eye. His white beard was soon
dark with blood.

With studied precision Slade kicked Moses just
above the crotch. The man let out a strangled gasp and
coiling over his scrotum tried to crawl away. Slade
thumb cocked his weapon and caught the back of the
old man's head in the barrel's sight. He toyed with the
idea of blowing away a little of the man's scalp. But he
wasn't that sure of his aim. Still. . . .

The blow came from his side at about the same time
he heard Turner's warning cry. It was Bolton.
Weaponless, the man had hurled himself at Slade,
burying his head in Slade's side and driving him
sharply back against one of the huge boulders that
bordered the water hole. It felt for a moment as if the
force of the Texan's thrust had broken one of his ribs.

He had trouble regaining his breath. As he slipped down the face of the boulder, he twisted away from Bolton, who was driving repeated, pistonlike blows to his head and chest.

By the time he had regained his feet and shaken off the ringing in his ears, the sheriff and Bridger had managed to grab Bolton from behind. There was a growing ache in the bridge of his nose and a painful swelling beginning in his upper lip. His rage building nicely, Slade watched Bolton struggle with silent fury to get loose; both men were having considerable difficulty hanging onto him.

He stepped in close and buried his fist deep into the tall man's midsection. The Texan jackknifed. Slade brought up his knee, catching Bolton in the face. The man sagged heavily forward. Turner and Bridger let him sprawl onto his face. Slade kicked him for a while, systematically, viciously, grunting heavily each time. When at last the Texan showed no response at all to his punishment, Slade bent over, grabbed the man by the back of his vest, dragged him to the edge of the pool, then lugged him still farther until his face fell into the water hole.

With his boot Slade pushed the Texan's head deep into the water. He waited until the tension in the man's neck relaxed and he saw bubbles breaking the surface of the pool before he yanked the man's head out of the water and then kicked him with such force that he went rolling down the slope beyond the water hole. As the Texan flipped lifelessly over and over down the treacherous, rock-strewn slope, Slade picked his six-gun and began pumping lead at the slowly receding figure. The whine of the ricocheting bullets filled the air. Slade did not stop until he had emptied his revolver. Then, his hands shaking, he proceeded to lift fresh bullets from his shellbelt and thumb them into the empty chambers.

A hand took his wrist firmly.

Slade looked up and saw Bridger standing close, an anxious frown on his face. "That's enough, Slade. You've killed him. You can stop now."

The look in Bridger's eyes made Slade pause. Bridger seemed deeply troubled, concerned rather. And for Slade.

Slade shook his hand free of Bridger, finished reloading his six-gun, then holstered it. He shuddered suddenly and shook himself involuntarily. Then he felt his face. His nose was pretty damn sore, but it was not broken. His lip, however, had continued to swell. It felt peculiar, like something alien that had crawled up onto his face and fastened itself there.

Deep anger stirred to life within him. He was not sorry he had killed the man. It was something Bolton had coming. That had already been decided, in fact.

He glanced then at Moses. The old man was on his feet, his legs braced wide apart. He was glowering over at Slade and had placed himself between Slade and the girl. Slade smiled thinly.

"You tried to kill us, old man. Poison us. You're lucky that isn't you down there. You better stop this foolishness or that girl behind you is going to start learning about men." Slade paused. "Or don't you think I am capable of that."

"You're capable, all right."

"Good. Then we understand each other. Get back to your horse. And you better get us to that canyon before dark."

"I can't promise you that."

"I said you'd better."

Moses started to walk back to the horses. Slade looked at Bridger and smiled. "Just lost my head a little back there," he told the man. "Nothing to get concerned about—but you better get your stomach in shape. There's a lot more of that coming, and you'll have to dig in like the rest of us."

"I know," the man said. He was still visibly shaken. "All of this . . . is more than I had bargained for." He frowned and looked back the way they had come. "I came out to this Godforsaken land for so many better reasons, or so I thought at the time."

Slade had no idea what the man was talking about, but it didn't matter. The only thing that mattered was that gold. If Bridger didn't have the stomach for what had to be done, well . . . that just meant Slade and the sheriff would have one less person to split it with.

Turner was looking down the embankment at the distant smudge that was the Texan's body. He turned to look at Slade.

"You want to check him out?" the sheriff asked. "He might still be alive."

"I hope he is. I've seen men die from wells poisoned by Apaches. He'll die slowly, if not from the poison, from his wounds. And the sun. Leave him. If he isn't dead, he soon will be."

When Parkhurst and the sheriff reached Moses, who had already mounted, Slade looked up at the old man. One side of his face was a dark, encrusted birthmark where the blood had coagulated. That side of his beard was a dark rust color.

"Who poisoned that well, old man—the Apaches?" Moses nodded.

"And you and Bolton knew it."

Again Moses nodded.

Slade looked back toward the slope and smiled. "Good," he said. "They always do a fine job when they fix a water hole, I hear."

The girl had mounted Bolton's horse. As Slade passed her, he saw her looking in the direction of the water hole. There were tears in her eyes. He smiled. She was not as cold—as untouched by all this—as she pretended.

"You'll be leading all four mules now, Marylou," Slade told her as he thrust the lead reins up into her hand. "You think you will be able to handle that?"

She looked at him for a long moment without replying. Then she nodded.

"Good."

As Slade stepped into his saddle a moment later, there was a smile on his face. The girl, he was certain, would come around. All in good time.

10

TIM HAD HEARD THE sound of shod hoofs on stone as Slade and the rest rode off. But he had been unable to move. As silence fell over the slope, he felt himself drifting off.

When he regained consciousness he found he was lying face up, his head turned away from the direct rays of the sun. The sun was low in the sky and his body was awash with perspiration. His neck and the side of his face had been cooked raw by the blazing sun. What had brought him around was the cooling shadow that kept passing between him and the sun.

And the sense that he was not alone.

Tim opened his eyes. A large buzzard was sitting on a boulder beside him. The great black bird was hunched forward, its bright eyes studying Tim patiently. The shadow had been another bird in the sky above swooping lower and lower. As the other buzzard swept past, the rush of air caused by its passage felt like a blast out of hell. Tim shuddered involuntarily and stirred, pushing himself to a sitting position. The buzzard's red, wrinkled head and neck quivered with indignation, its long, hooked bill opening slightly.

Tim's right hand closed about a rock. He grabbed it convulsively and flung it at the loathsome bird. He missed. The bird lifted up on its ungainly legs, reluctantly tottered from the boulder, then flung itself headlong down the slope, its great wings opening and carrying it in suddenly graceful fashion into the air. Tim glanced up. The other buzzard was soaring high overhead in ever-widening circles.

Painfully, Tim struggled to his feet. He felt battered and broken. Still, everything seemed in working order—the hinges bent maybe and the bolts loosened some, but nothing bad enough to keep him where he was. That was important. Somehow, he had to overtake Slade and the others. Once Slade and Turner found that gold, there would be no reason for them to let Moses live or to leave Marylou alone.

His face was swollen and one eye almost shut. Slade's knee had loosened some of his teeth and split his lip, and the fall had bruised his back and thighs, but none of his ribs had been broken—and not a single bullet had found his body. He had had enough wits left to keep from swallowing the water he had let into his mouth, and when he was bouncing down the slope he had managed to spit it all out of his mouth.

He would not get sick then, but he would have to emulate the Apache if he were to overtake Slade, since he no longer had a horse. He found his hat and climbed back up toward the trail they had been following.

The sun was rapidly sinking lower. When he turned his head to glance at it, he felt the sunburned portion of his neck protest. The sun had doubled in size by this time and was hanging like a bloodshot eye just above the mountains to the west. He regained the trail. There was plenty of sign for him to follow—even through the night, if it came to that, since the moon would be full.

He started off, walking as rapidly as he could.

The moon had not yet risen and he was stumbling with almost every step. The uneven ground was more than a chore. It was a tortuous trial. More than once he twisted his ankle. It was the heels on his boots, he knew. As he had found out once before over this same punishing terrain—boots were for riding, not walking.

The moon rose at last, peeking over a butte off to his right, yellow and flat, casting a silvery blue sheen over the ground before him. The mules' tracks and the imprint of the horses' hoofs jumped into clear relief.

Tim stopped, leaned his aching frame back against a high boulder and bent to the task of pulling off his boots. It took some doing. His feet were so swollen he was afraid for a moment or two that he would never be able to free his aching feet from their prison. Holding the boots in each hand, Tim started up again, picking his way carefully. For a while the cool ground was a welcome change for his sweaty, aching feet.

But only for a while.

He could not see well enough to avoid all the sharp rocks that littered the trail. He began to open cuts in his feet. Soon, every step took another notch out of them. It was like walking on straight razors. The moon was high above him when at last he stumbled painfully to a halt and rested with his back against a wall of rock.

He looked back the way he had come. A trail of bloody footprints stood out sharply in the moonlight. He looked down at his feet. They were throbbing painfully, which was precisely what they should have been doing, considering their condition. As Tim watched, a puddle of blood grew slowly under them.

He leaned his head back so that he could not see his bleeding feet. So far, he had managed to cover quite a distance. But he could hardly walk much further with his feet in this condition. And he had no water. Despite the chill desert night, he was dry, his lips cracked for want of moisture. Tomorrow would be as mercilessly bright and sunny and as fearsomely hot as today had been.

The Apaches, he knew, could travel enormous distances on foot over this kind of terrain. It was their moccasins. Their famous, thigh-length moccasins. He remembered the soft, steady pit-pat of the Apache that carried him through the night to their camp. Closing his eyes, he saw again the Apaches dancing, their high moccasins plunging down without concern for the uneven, rocky ground.

Unbidden, the face of the old medicine man appeared before his mind's eye. The old man's prunelike face leaned close and he smiled his gap-toothed smile. Sibilant words about not worrying—about not being concerned that he had not been with his father when he entered that saloon—came to him without warning. Confused images, nightmarish actions, flooded over him. He found himself trying to remember what had happened to him in that Apache camp.

He shook his head, frustrated at his lack of success, and shivered. He became aware of how cold he was. Only his feet were warm. They fairly sizzled, he commented to himself ironically.

His only sane recourse, he felt now, was to put the boots back on. Pinch though they might, he could not go another step on these bloody stumps. He had clung to the boots and placed them down beside him when he slumped to the ground. He reached for them now and began to tug the right one on.

He could not do it. The foot had swollen incredibly. All he succeeded in doing was to fill the boot with his blood. He hurled it from him furiously.

Again the face of the old medicine man appeared before him.

Tim frowned, looked down at his feet, then swiftly shrugged out of his vest. In a moment he had his shirt off. His undershirt came next. Both were filthy, stained dark, and heavy with perspiration. He began ripping the top of his long johns and his shirt into strips. . . .

In less than an hour Tim had fashioned his own moccasins by wrapping his feet carefully in the strips of cloth he had salvaged from his shirt and undershirt. Gingerly, he got to his feet and took a step. There was some discomfort, but nothing like there had been earlier. His feet looked twice their normal size and ridiculously clumsy because of the way he had been forced to knot the strips of cloth.

But he could walk. Smiling, he started off again. He was tired—exhausted, really—but he would travel another couple of miles or so before resting again. He was confident now that he would overtake Slade.

He began to walk faster.

Moses took a deep breath as he looked around. They had camped outside the canyon's entrance the night before. Now, in the full blaze of morning's light, he found himself surveying a canyon Naretena and his warriors had kept him out of for the last year. This canyon was, he knew without a doubt, the source of their gold dust. Moses had come so close. It made his mouth dry to think of what might have been.

As he rode slowly through the narrow defile that opened into the canyon, he saw the tawny, sheer walls of rock lifting up on both sides. Ahead of him the vista widened considerably. The canyon was a winding cut in the earth that went on for miles and was known, at least to the few prospectors Moses had consulted, for its treacherous bypaths and smaller canyons that branched off the main one. After awhile—and especially under the influence of a maddening sun—all the rocks began to look alike, exits became entrances, walls appeared where before there had been vistas, and sand grew where lush grass to feed a man's burro had been confidently expected.

No one truly knew this place—except perhaps the Apaches, Moses realized as he rode on into the canyon and gazed about him. The smooth walls were broken by strata of umber-colored rock. Great fractures undercut the walls in places, their cavelike interiors hidden in blue shadow. A shallow stream cut its way along the pale sandy floor.

Moses saw the tracks then, etched in the sand close to the stream. There had been rain more than once this past month, but it had not been enough, evidently, to wash out all of the tracks Bart and those heavily-laden mules had left. Turner saw the tracks at the same moment Moses did.

"Hey! Look there!" he cried, spurring his horse ahead of Moses.

Moses pulled up and watched as the sheriff splashed through the shallow stream, dismounted swiftly, and went down on one knee to examine the sign.

It didn't take him long to make certain that these were the tracks belonging to Burt Talbot and his men. The sheriff stood up and beckoned to them excitedly.

"You were right, Slade!" he called. "We don't need Bolton! Just follow these tracks!"

Bridger and Slade spurred past Moses and got down beside him to inspect the sign. As Moses splashed across the stream and pulled up beside them, Bridger turned to look up at him.

"I remember Bolton telling me that one of the mules was lame." He pointed then to one of the tracks. "There's the one."

"Look at the depth of them tracks," said the sheriff, his voice almost hushed. "Them animals were sure loaded down some. And that's a fact."

"If Bart got all of it," Bridger agreed.

Slade looked at the agent. "How much, Bridger? You never did let that out."

"Fifty-thousand, give or take a couple of hundred."

Slade looked quickly at the sheriff. Their eyes registered surprise, then a swift resolve. Moses sensed in both men a quickening of their appetite—their lust, rather—for the gold. Hells bells, he felt it himself. Fifty-thousand would buy a lot of fancy duds for Marylou—and some fine boots and a set of new teeth for him. And that would be just for starters.

"Well then," said the sheriff, "what the hell are we standing around here for? Let's get on with it!"

He vaulted into his saddle, Slade and Bridger following his example. Bridger almost lost his big white Stetson in his eagerness. Soon the three of them were splashing along through the shallow water, following the tracks, Moses sticking close behind them.

He glanced back at Marylou. She was still leading the four mules, her face impassive. Yet as his glance steadied on her eyes, he thought he caught a glimmer of something that surprised him—angry resolve, it seemed like. Maybe she was coming out of it. Could be that Bolton had managed to drive out them evil spirits the Apaches said had come to live in her head.

He turned back around. The sheriff was in the lead, and they were making good time, he thought glumly. He had hoped to be able to stall them somehow, even get them lost perhaps in one of them narrow canyons—lead them on a merry chase until either Bolton caught up with them—or Naretena returned. He could not believe that Bolton was really dead. Not that man. There was just something about him that would not let him believe such a thing. Maybe he was a fool, but he felt it anyway.

His groin was still sore where Slade had kicked him and the side of his head felt like it didn't belong to him. God knows what Slade would have done to him if Bolton hadn't jumped the gambler when he did.

No, Bolton was not dead. Moses Kelly refused to believe that.

The sheriff had pulled up in the center of the canyon. The stream they had been following had cut sharply right into a smaller canyon. The floor of the canyon now was almost pure cap rock. And there was no sign left to follow. As Moses brought his horse to a halt beside Slade, Turner spurred his horse into the smaller canyon, calling to them that he would be back within a few minutes.

The four of them waited.

It was close to a quarter of an hour, Moses judged, before the sheriff galloped back into the main canyon.

"Nothing!" he shouted as he galloped near. "Not a single goddamned track!"

As Turner's horse slowed to a halt, all three men turned as one to face Moses.

"Well, old man," said Slade. "It shouldn't be far from here then. Where's that mine shaft?"

"Like I told you, there's more than one mine shaft in this here place. It ain't goin' to be easy finding the right one."

"Take us to the nearest one. Now."

Moses frowned and looked carefully around him. "Well now, let me see. It's been some time. Don't know's I can be absolutely sure just where I am now."

Slade nudged his horse close alongside Moses's mount. "How many did you say there were altogether, Moses?"

"Mine shafts?"

"That's right."

"Oh, seven maybe."

"You said closer to ten at the cabin."

"Ten then." Moses frowned. He was trying to remember if he had said anything of the sort.

By the time he realized he had never given them a specific number, Slade had brought his right arm around in a sweeping arc that caught Moses under his chin and sent him flying backward off his mount. He landed hard on his back. Dazed, he watched as Slade dismounted and stood over him.

"You're a liar, Moses."

"I don't remember how many they were, damn you!" Moses said.

Slade kicked him in the side, his boot digging in so far that Moses thought a Chinaman's firecracker had exploded inside his gut. He began to crawl away. Slade reached down and hauled him to his feet. Moses tried, but he couldn't stand upright.

"I'm going to keep punishing you, old man, until you tell me the truth. Punish you—or punish the girl." He glanced up at Marylou sitting her horse beside them. "You wouldn't mind that, now would you."

Her face showed nothing, but Moses saw her fingers tighten on the reins that held the mules.

"There were two mines that I know of," Moses said.

Slade slapped Moses, hard. "How many?"

"Two!"

"How many?"

"I told you!"

"You said seven, then you said ten—now you say two. How can I believe you, old man?"

He reached for the bridle to Marylou's mount, a cruel smile on his face. Moses saw the pure devilment in the man's cold eyes and shuddered.

"All right, damn you! There ain't but one."

"Take us to it."

"Yes," said the sheriff, leaning over his saddle horn as he looked down at Moses. "And hurry it up!" The sheriff looked at Slade. "Damned if I didn't believe the old sonofabitch the first time!"

Slade laughed as he vaulted into his saddle. "That's why you make such a lousy poker player, Turner. You never watch the eyes. I do."

It took a while for Moses to climb into his saddle and no one reached over to help him. At last he settled himself gingerly onto the saddle and nudged his mare into the lead.

For better than two hours they rode, following the canyon's winding, snaking course. The sheer walls occasionally fell away as they crossed open stretches of sand and cap rock. But they would soon close in on them again, their striated faces hanging menacingly over them as they rode through blue shadow, the sky but a sliver of bright blue high overhead.

At last they rode into a broad, fairly open stretch and ahead of them Moses saw, scattered close around a low shoulder of rock beside which a thin trickle of a stream wandered, the skeletons of four large animals. At once he knew they were the remains of Bart Talbot's mules.

Slade, Turner, and Bridger saw them at the same time Moses did and rode ahead of him and dismounted to inspect the remains. By the time Moses reached them, Turner had pulled out of one of the rib cages a single Apache's typically small arrow.

He held it up for Moses and the others to see.

"Apache," Moses said quietly, as he reined in. "Naretena's band, most likely."

Moses looked around then. The four skeletons were a bright white in the blazing sun. So clean in fact had the bones been picked that not a fly buzzed over them and not a bird could be seen hopping about within their bleached rib cages. The haunches, Moses noticed, were missing, and that made sense. The Apaches were not going to pass up fresh meat, even if it were mule.

Slade squinted up at Moses. "We're getting near, old man. That right?"

Moses nodded. "Them's Talbot's mules, what's left of 'em. So I guess we are."

He looked ahead of him, across the canyon floor. There were three arroyos leading from this place. If Moses were not mistaken, and he did not think he was, the left one led further into Diablo Canyon—and the mine shaft he had started to work. He had told Tim the Apaches had caught him panning a stream as an

instinctive precaution, but the truth was they had
found him shoring up a mine shaft on his way in—he
was certain—to the mother lode.

Digging his heels into the mare's flanks, he crossed
the shallow stream and started toward the arroyo,
Marylou keeping right behind him. The others
mounted up quickly and followed. The arroyo was so
narrow they had to ride through it single file. They
dropped rapidly as red dirt and loose rock showered
down on them whenever they brushed the walls.
Finally the arroyo spilled out onto a sloping, massive
cap rock that rested on the floor of the canyon, which
stretched a quarter mile or more ahead of them, then
bent in a sharp, S-turn to their right, curving around,
lost to sight behind the towering walls.

Moses recognized it all. The mine shaft was behind
that first turn.

He clattered across the rock, the others surging
around him and keeping pace, glancing nervously,
eagerly, at him as they rode. Their lust for the gold was
like a smell they were giving off.

Moses rounded the canyon wall and cantered just
ahead of them, his glance searching the rock face ahead
of him. Only there was no rock face. And where the
mine shaft should have been, huge boulders were piled,
as if by some massive, careless hand. He pulled up and
looked around. Could he have chosen the wrong
arroyo back there?

Frowning, he studied the slope. His inner eye kept
trying to superimpose on it the features his memory
told him should have been there. He glanced up, his
gaze taking in the familiar light and dark strata, then
the ledge high above. Yes, there was that lone juniper.
He looked back down at the base of the canyon wall
where the mine shaft should have been.

But the mine shaft was gone.

Slade pulled his horse up beside Moses. The others reined in on the other side of him. It was Slade who spoke first.

"Well, what are you waiting for, old man?"

"Damn you!" Moses suddenly exploded, turning on the gambler furiously. "Don't keep calling me an old man!"

Slade's eyes narrowed speculatively. He seemed to be measuring just how far he could still push Moses. He eased back in his saddle and smiled. There was no honest warmth in it, but it was a smile. He had decided to back off—for now, anyway. "Pardon my lack of courtesy," he said, with mock gallantry. "But we are all anxiously waiting for you to lead us on to that mine shaft. You can understand our eagerness, I am sure."

"I understand it, all right."

Moses looked again at the now unfamiliar rock face and came to a quick decision.

"We ain't there yet, and we got a ways to go. I'm just getting my bearings now," he said. "You'll have to slow your blood down a mite."

He clapped his heels to the mare's flank and rode on past where the mine shaft should have been, the rest following. There should be another arroyo up ahead, he realized, sweat standing out on his forehead. If there wasn't the jig would be up—and even his desperate hope to get Marylou free of them would be doomed.

He rode about fifty yards farther before he saw it, just as he had expected. It was there ahead of him, a deep cleft in an otherwise solid wall of rock. He looked back. Marylou was keeping pace with him; the rest were strung out behind. Slade and the sheriff were riding side by side, Bridger behind them. Moses glanced at Marylou.

With a quick nod of his head, he indicated that she should ride on ahead of him into the draw. The sudden alertness in her eyes told him she understood. She spurred past him. As she did so, he took the four leads for the mules from her. Marylou was frowning as she left him with the mules and galloped into the draw.

Moses spurred after her. As the cool, shadowed walls of the draw closed about him, he heard Slade's shout. It would be Slade who noticed first, Moses thought, as he dropped the mules' leads and roweled his mare furiously.

"Make a break for it, Marylou!" he called to her.

She glanced back over her shoulder at him, her face a pale, startled flower in the dimness of the narrow place.

"Go on!" Moses cried. "This is your chance!"

A shot rang out, its echo and the ricochet of the bullet filling the draw with violent sound. Moses lowered his head and galloped after Marylou. She was well ahead of him now and after a sudden turn was out of sight. Moses looked back. In the confined space of the draw, the four mules were effectively blocking Slade and the sheriff. Moses caught a glimpse of them trying first to ride around the suddenly stolid animals and then through them.

Moses saw Slade's horse suddenly rise up on its haunches, its front legs pawing at the air. Then Slade was tumbling backward off the animal, which lurched over onto him, whinnying frantically. With the sheriff and Bridger bottled up behind Slade, Moses was able to lengthen the distance between them rapidly.

Soon he and Marylou were through the draw. Abruptly, Marylou pulled up. Moses overtook her and saw what had stopped her. They were on a ledge. Below it a great fissure, a ragged rip in the earth's mantle, cut down through the layered red rock toward the shadowed depths of what appeared to be another canyon.

The drop to the floor of that canyon was better than a hundred feet, and no safe way down even on foot.

Moses looked back to the slope off to his left. It was one of the ways he had come here once before. They would have to leave their mounts and scramble up on foot. Moses glanced back. Somehow, Bridger had managed to ride around the mules and Slade's downed horse. He was urging his horse on through the draw at almost a gallop.

"Off the horse!" he told Marylou, "and get up that slope! Hurry!"

She slid out of the saddle and started up the slope with a swiftness Moses immediately envied as he eased himself out of his own saddle and started after her. The footing was atrocious. Rocks he needed for support came loose under his grasp. The gravel under his boots gave way. He found himself sliding down the slope almost as often as he made progress up it. It was a nightmare and when he had progressed only a quarter of the way up, he saw how futile it all was—at least for him. A moment before he had lost his sombrero.

He steadied himself and looked back and watched the sombrero tumble down toward the draw just as Bridger rode out of it, shading his eyes with his hand as he looked up the slope at him and at Marylou who was not far above Moses.

Moses turned and looked back up at the girl. "Keep on going!" he called to her.

She stopped and looked down at him.

"I said keep on going!"

She hesitated only an instant then turned about and continued the steep climb. In a moment or two she was out of sight behind a precariously perched boulder.

Moses looked back down at Bridger. The agent had his revolver out, but seemed somewhat hesitant to use it.

"I'm coming down!" Moses said. "You don't have to fire that thing!"

"Come on down then," Bridger called.

The agent did not holster his weapon, however, and kept it trained on Moses all during his painful, lurching scramble back down the slope. Moses reached level ground just beside the mounted Bridger only a few seconds before Slade, back aboard his horse, rode out of the draw. The look in Slade's eyes told Moses that his situation was desperate. Desperate action, then, was necessary. Moses Kelly was not going to let that sonofabitching card player kick him around any more.

As Bridger glanced carelessly back at the approaching gambler, Moses reached up and grabbed Bridger's gun hand, and yanked. The agent was too startled by the action to brace himself and toppled forward out of his saddle with an ease that Moses had not been prepared to handle. The agent crashed heavily down upon Moses, causing the old prospector to buckle under him.

Moses still held Bridger's gun hand, and as he went down, he wrested the gun out of Bridger's grasp. Bridger rolled frantically off Moses and Moses found himself flat on his back, the rear of his head wedged in between two large rocks. Slade, still in the saddle, loomed above Moses. His revolver was out, its gleaming barrel pointed at Moses.

"Let loose of that gun, old man," Slade said, smiling thinly.

"Don't shoot him, Slade!" Bridger cried. "He hasn't shown us that mine shaft yet!"

"Then take that gun out of his hand," snapped Slade.

"No!" Moses heard himself cry. "Damn you! Damn all of you! I ain't going to show any of you that mine shaft." He laughed then. "You sonsabitches! It's gone! That's right, gone!"

Slade looked uncertainly at Bridger. The sheriff rode up then, his own six-gun out, and pulled up beside Slade.

"What the hell's he saying?" the sheriff wanted to know.

"Says the mine shaft's gone," Slade reported, his voice cold. "Guess we're going to have to beat it out of him." He glanced up the slope. "And that girl's gone, too. I call that a real shame."

"She won't last long out here," said the sheriff, looking back down at Moses. "You better call her back."

No, Moses would not call her back. She had a fighting chance now. With these animals she would have no chance at all. And Moses had no chance with these men either. Slade would do his best to beat the information he wanted out of him. He would never believe that Moses simply did not know where the mine shaft was, that his memory seemed to have failed him. He would prefer not to believe it. He would rather just keep on beating on Moses. It was the kind of work that really pleasured him.

Slowly, deliberately, Moses brought up the revolver he had taken from Bridger. Slade frowned in surprise and reined his horse back hastily.

"Don't be a fool, old man! I'll kill you!"

"Then do it!" Moses cried, lifting the gun in an effort to fix the gambler in the barrel's sight.

He thumbcocked it clumsily and for an instant the

sight wavered over Slades' startled face. Slade didn't wait for Moses to steady his aim. He fired twice down at him. Moses felt the impact of each slug as it ripped into his chest. At the same moment he felt the revolver bucking in his hand as he squeezed off his one shot. Before he could cock the revolver a second time, the weapon fell from his hands. Untouched, Slade still loomed over him, regarding him through narrowed eyes as he holstered his weapon.

Moses did not care that he had not hit Slade. Marylou had gotten away. It was strange, but he felt no pain—only an enormous weight gathering on his chest, like death was sitting there. The shattering echo of the three gunshots faded, as did the sound of the horses' nervous shuffling, the faces looking down....

Someone picked up his sombrero and placed it over his face.

11

THE OMINOUS RATTLE OF gunfire behind her stopped
Marylou in her tracks. Well away from the lip of the
canyon by this time, she turned and ran back, her
thick-soled moccasins serving her well as she covered
the broken terrain. She reached the canyon and peered
down the slope. A rock wren, startled, darted up before
her and flew off, scolding as it went.

She saw Moses then. He was lying on his back on
the ledge far below her, his sombrero over his head. He
was lying so still, so very still, that she knew at once
Moses was dead. The others were riding back into the
draw without even a backward glance.

She sat suddenly down and let the tears come.
Moses was dead! He had been so kind to her. Gruff at
times, yes. Demanding. But he had let her alone, let her
heal. He had treated her as he would have his own
daughter, firmly, but with patience—and love. Saving
her had been all he wanted—and it had cost him his
life!

The enormity of it shook her powerfully, battered

her like a storm. She bowed her face in her hands and sobbed. She sobbed until she wanted to sob no more—until an icy, angry clarity took hold of her mind. She looked around her at a world she seemed to be seeing for the first time. Hiding from this world and its evil was no good. It didn't work. You could not escape that way. You had to fight back!

Without flinching, she saw again the *rurales*, saw them surrounding her father's wagon, scratching and grinning, their guttural laughter exploding whenever their obscene eyes caught her peering out from behind her father. She saw her father, shotgun in hand, stepping down from the wagon and approaching the one who appeared to be their leader. He was a squat, heavily-armed man with two wide cartridge belts crossing his chest, his face covered with a thick, wiry beard. His enormous sombrero was pushed back off his head and a red-flowered bandanna was tied like a cap over his skull. He looked like a mounted pirate, she had thought.

Her father suddenly stepped back, obviously angry at some demand of the *rurale* leader. The bearded leader laughed then, obviously delighted that he had provoked such a reaction. Two shots almost in unison and then a third and a fourth erupted from all sides. She saw her father, still on his feet, being shaken as if by a violent wind as the bullets punched into his body.

She remembered screaming and plunging out of the wagon to her father's side, and then the hands were on her, all over her, clutching, grabbing, ripping her dress, forcing her down. Stubbly, grinning faces scraped her face and neck raw as they grunted over her. Sitting there now, she remembered—forced herself to re-member—the searing pain of their clumsy penetrations, the screams that seemed not to be a part of her, the slow disengagement of her mind from the rest of her, the floating off into a world without feeling, where she heard without hearing, saw without seeing, touched without touching anything at all. It was a dim netherworld where she had fled to be safe and had remained, trapped, until Moses, and finally Tim, had shown her the way out. . . .

Now they, too, had been taken from her. Would she run and hide again and let only a tiny part of her peep out at a world gone mad? No! Not this time!

Marylou got to her feet, took one last look down the slope at the still body of Moses Kelly, then turned and began to run back across the ground she had covered earlier. Far below her, the three riders would be forced to follow the canyon's winding, twisting course. She intended to stay above the canyon, to run straight and perhaps overtake them.

Twice she fell, but each time she was back on her feet almost as soon as she hit. She became aware, after the second fall, of warm blood on one knee, but paid it no heed. Perspiration had plastered her blouse to her breasts and her buckskin skirt was heavy with it when she pulled up before one of the canyon's loops. With awesome suddenness it had opened before her. She was panting deeply, sucking in air in sharp, painful gasps. The ground had already begun to tip crazily under her plunging feet. She went down on her hands and knees, her head down, and waited until the ground steadied and she could breathe without gasping.

She was feeling much better when the hollow chock of hoofs on stone echoed in the canyon below. She scrambled to her feet and looked down. Slade was just emerging from around a bend in the canyon. In a moment the sheriff and the other one appeared, leading the four mules and the two riderless horses.

She waited until they were almost below her before she shouted down to them and waved her arms.

Slade was the first to see her. He pulled up and, turning, pointed her out to the others. They halted also.

"Don't leave me!" she cried. "Take me with you!"

She saw Slade's teeth gleaming in his dark face as he smiled up at her. "Will you be nice?" he called. The word "nice" echoed mockingly up and down the canyon.

"Of course!" she yelled back. "But how do I get down?"

Slade put his hand behind him on the cantle to steady himself as he peered around at the canyon's rim. Then he pointed to a spot ahead of Marylou, about fifty yards farther along the rim.

"There's a trail there! You can make it—!"

She ran along the edge of the canyon until she found the trail. It was narrow and followed a cleft that seemed to have opened in the canyon wall. The trail itself seemed to have been worn smooth by tiny hoofs. It was a game trail.

She started down.

Since mid-morning Tim had been alternately running and walking above the canyon. When he passed the trail he had used that moonlit night to descend to the valley floor after Bart Talbot, he knew he must be getting close to overtaking Slade and the others. Their tracks had been visible from the moment they entered the canyon, etched clearly in the sand and clay beside the stream that meandered down the center of the winding canyon.

A draw opened before him, slanting down toward the canyon below. Tim decided to take it; now was the time, he felt, to get closer to the floor of the canyon. A few yards farther down the draw opened into a fissure, a ragged rip knifing through the layered red rocks to the shadowed canyon floor. To keep going down, Tim found himself jumping from ledge to ledge. He dropped rapidly.

Abruptly the draw spilled out onto a ledge. At this point the canyon twisted sharply back to his left and the ledge thrust out into the turn like the prow of a ship. Kneeling on the edge of it, Tim peered over. Below the ledge there was a shallow pool fed by the stream that was now but a thin blade of water meandering through the canyon. The pool reflected the bright blue of the sky. In flood the stream undoubtedly swept against the cliff wall below him. The wall, facing that swift sweep of water over the ages, was now deeply undercut, forming a great open-faced cavern. Sizable blocks and slabs of rust-colored rocks had broken off and tumbled into the pool and onto the canyon floor near the bend of the stream.

The drop from the ledge to the pool was better than sixty feet. This was not the way down. He retreated from the ledge, found a crack in the canyon wall as broad as a roadway that slanted down. He followed it until he was confronted by a five- or six-foot fissure running at a right angle to the crack. He would have to leap over it to keep going. He backed up, raced to the edge and leaped. He was going downhill, and if his feet were not so sore, he would have made it easily. As it was, he fell short and caught himself with his forearms, cracking them smartly when he hit.

He hauled himself out and continued on. Not long after, his stone roadway became a narrow ledge thrusting out over a narrow arroyo leading into the canyon. The drop from here to the floor of the arroyo was much less than from the ledge above, but it was at least fifteen feet, he guessed, and the ground was littered with broken slabs of rust-colored rock.

Still, this was considerably better than sixty feet. And when he saw how fresh the tracks were under this ledge, it decided him.

They had taken his six-gun but left him his cartridge belt. He unbuckled it, looped it through the buckle and fitted the loop around a tusklike projection of rock that poked out over the lip of the ledge. Almost three feet of the belt hung now below the ledge. That would help some. If he could swing on the belt, he might be able to select a less rock-strewn spot on which to come down.

He was testing the belt when he heard the distant clop of shod hoofs on stone. They were returning up this arroyo. Unarmed, he was a dead man if they caught sight of him on this ledge—or attempting to get down. Swiftly, he dropped below the ledge and swung into the narrow, shadowed arroyo. He was at the end of the belt soon, but could see down only with difficulty. He didn't really have that much of a choice anyway, he realized. He kicked off, braced himself, and came down hard, his flailing feet striking the wall first, then crushing down into a gravelly mixture of stone and loose soil at the base of the wall. He sank in up to his ankles, then pulled himself free. His shin was bleeding, but outside of that he was unhurt.

The sound of hoofbeats was echoing loudly now in the narrow arroyo, but no horsemen were visible yet. Keeping low, Tim ran further into the narrow draw, heading for a great, crouching boulder behind which he might be able to find cover.

What he would do then would depend on circumstances. The only thing he had going he realized, was the element of surprise. It was not much, perhaps, but it would have to do.

As soon as they rode into the arroyo, Marylou knew that the time had come for her to make her move. It was Slade she wanted. He must have been the one who killed Moses. After all, she had seen him kill Tim. To get Slade, then, would be enough. She had no illusions; with Slade dead, she would be at the mercy of the others. But that did not matter.

For at last, she was going to fight back!

Marylou was astride Tim's horse and—as she had forseen—Slade had told her to ride beside him. His suggestive smiles had curdled her insides, but she had hidden from him the fury in her eyes by ducking her head whenever he looked at her. He had seemed greatly encouraged by that reaction.

Her plan was simple enough. As soon as the walls of the arroyo forced them to ride closer together, she would snatch his gleaming pistol from its holster and shoot him with it.

"Damn it!" cursed the sheriff. He was riding well to the rear, with Bridger between Marylou and him. "Now that Moses and Bolton're dead, we'll never find that gold!" the sheriff continued. "You're too damn quick with that gun, Slade!"

Slade glanced back at the sheriff, his eyes hard. "That's right, Turner. I am fast with this gun. Make sure you don't forget that."

"Now there's no sense in talking like that," the sheriff protested, his voice no longer strident. "But what are we going to do? How're we going to find that gold now?"

"That mine shaft's around here someplace. We'll find it."

Bridger spoke up then, his voice gloomy. "I wonder. This endeavor has been hounded by ill-luck from the start. I am beginning to wonder if it is not a sign of God's wrath."

"A *what?*" Slade seemed astonished at this remark. He turned in his saddle to look squarely at Bridger. "What is this, Bridger? All of a sudden you're a goddamn preacher?"

The man seemed to recoil, as if Slade's words had struck deep. The fellow shook his head. Marylou caught a glimpse of some inner torment in the man's eyes. She was surprised also. This man was no better than the others, judging from his actions. Yet he seemed suddenly vulnerable.

She hardened her resolve. No. He was no more vulnerable, no more human than the other two. If she got the chance she would kill him as well. And the sheriff.

She looked ahead of her. The arroyo was narrowing finally. Her heart began to beat faster and she felt cold sweat standing out on her forehead. What had seemed so easy when she had imagined it was now no longer so simple a task. Kill Bridger and the sheriff? She would be lucky to kill Slade.

Her resolve hardened as Slade's horse and hers began to ride closer. Slade glanced at her, the trace of a smile on his face. "It's getting pretty tight in here, Marylou," he told. "Maybe you better hold up and ride behind me."

She ducked her head, as if in acknowledgement of the wisdom of his suggestion. But she did not rein in the horse. She rode a few yards farther on. Her thigh and that of Slade's were almost touching.

He glanced at her again. She knew he was about to repeat his suggestion again, perhaps not as pleasantly as before. Before he opened his mouth, she stood in her left stirrup and snatched the butt of his revolver and withdrew the weapon. It came so easily, she was startled. But its weight appalled her. She had no idea a handgun could be this heavy.

Slade's reaction was instant. As Marylou struggled to bring up the weapon to fire it, Slade knocked her backward off her horse with a single sweeping blow. She heard herself cry out in surprise as she landed heavily on her back. Yet she clung to the revolver and found herself staring up at the still mounted Slade. She raised the revolver. She did not see how she could miss at this range. She pulled the trigger.

Nothing happened!

She tugged frantically on the trigger. What was wrong?

"Shoot her!" cried Slade to Bridger. "Before she cocks it!"

Slade himself was pulling his carbine from the saddle boot. Only now she knew what was wrong! Holding the revolver with both hands, she forced back the hammer.

"I can't shoot her!" Bridger cried. "I won't! We have killed enough!"

Out of the corner of her eye, Marylou saw Bridger fling down his weapon. It clattered heavily among the rocks behind her. She ignored it, however, as she brought up the revolver a second time even as Slade levered a cartridge into the carbine's firing chamber.

Steadying the revolver with both hands she squeezed the trigger. The gun discharged with a kick and a roar so awesome she was flung back and the gun went flying from her hand. She saw Slade's hat fly back off his head as his horse reared under him. Stunned, she lay back among the rocks. The gun was gone now and she had missed.

"No!" cried Bridger. "No, Slade. Don't kill her! She's unarmed!"

Slade's face was shiny white in the shadowed arroyo, a mask of fury. He raised the carbine carefully to his shoulder. Marylou closed her eyes and waited for the bullet's impact.

The sudden shouting brought Tim from around the boulder. He had been crouching in wait, gathering himself to pounce as soon as Slade passed him. It would have been a desperate, perhaps futile, move, yet as far as he could figure, it was the only course open to him.

Now all that was changed.

He was running down the arroyo toward them when he heard Bridger shout something and fling down his revolver. Then the shot came from the ground and Slade's horse reared momentarily. The man's hat tumbled to the ground in front of him and Tim trampled it as he ran.

Bridger was crying out to Slade not to shoot. But Slade was coolly aiming his carbine at someone on the ground behind him. He was twisted about in his saddle and his horse, still uneasy from the shot, was making it difficult for the man to aim.

It was all the time Tim needed. He swept alongside Slade's horse, reached up and snatched the rifle from the man's grasp, barrel first. He looked then and saw that it was Marylou he had been aiming at. She was flat on her back in the middle of the arroyo, staring in amazement up at him.

Tim swung to face Slade. But the man uttered a cry and spurred his horse on down the arroyo. Tim was about to raise the rifle to fire at him, but heard a revolver being cocked behind him. He swung around, sinking to one knee as he did so, and saw the sheriff hauling up his big Colt.

As Tim brought the carbine up to his shoulder, the sheriff fired. The bullet stung Tim's face with shards of rock from a boulder beside him. Tim flinched away momentarily, then steadied his aim and squeezed off a shot. The bullet struck Turner solidly in the chest, just above the heart. Tim saw the tiny spurt of dust erupt where the bullet entered. Turner sagged back, coughed and slid sideways from the saddle. His revolver struck before he did, clattering among the rocks.

Tim swung the carbine around to cover Bridger.

The man flung both his hands into the air. "Don't shoot!" the man cried, "for the love of God!"

Tim looked down then at Marylou. "You all right?"

She nodded. "I thought you were dead. Slade shot you. You were lying so still."

"Slade missed. I was lucky."

"I wanted to kill him. I wanted to kill Slade."

He frowned at her. She seemed ... so much better. All this had transformed her, it seemed. It had shaken her out of herself. She spoke of wanting to kill Slade. Anger had done it. Fury at Slade and all that he stood for. He smiled. It had been what had kept him going, as well.

He reached down and gave her his hand to help her up. He saw Slade's gun then, gleaming brightly on the ground behind her. He reached past her and took it in his hands, hefting it. A fine weapon. But he had no belt or holster. He handed it to her.

"Keep this," he told her, "in case Bridger tries anything. I'll go see to the sheriff." And then he paused, suddenly troubled. "Where's Moses?"

"He's dead," she replied. "They killed him."

Tim glanced in sudden fury up at Bridger.

"It was Slade!" the man cried. "I had nothing to do with it! He killed him. The old man had a gun!"

A great weariness settled over Tim. He looked back at Marylou. "Where is he?"

"They left him back there."

"They didn't bury him? They just left him for the buzzards?"

She nodded, her head suddenly bowing, tears coursing down her cheeks. Tim looked back up at Bridger.

"Get down off that horse and see to your partner," he told him. "And let me have your gunbelt."

The agent scrambled down off his horse and did as Tim directed. Then he hastened back to where the sheriff lay. Before Tim followed Bridger, he picked up the man's discarded weapon and dropped it into his holster. He withdrew it a couple of times to note its heft and balance, then turned to Marylou, satisfied.

"We'll go back for Moses," he told her. "Do you know the way?"

"I . . . think I do."

"We'll find it then. These tracks won't be difficult to follow."

She nodded.

He looked into her eyes and was pleased, once again, at what he found there. There was fear in them—anger and sorrow, as well—but it was under control. As she had told him back at Moses's cabin when they were getting the water, *it is like a part of me has come out of darkness.* He had been afraid the events that followed that admission might have pushed her back into darkness. Apparently, they hadn't. It *was* going to be all right now.

He left her then to see about the sheriff.

Turner was dying. On one knee beside him, Tim examined the wound. The bullet had entered only inches above the heart and then raised hell inside before punching out through his back. The hole there was as big as Tim's fist. Blood was trickling from one corner of the sheriff's mouth, and he was coughing raggedly.

"He's a dead man, Bridger. You stay with him. I'm going back to bury Moses."

The man nodded. His lips had been moving silently all during Tim's inspection of Turner's wound. "I must get something," he muttered.

Tim got to his feet and watched the man hurry back to his horse. Out of his saddlebag he fished what looked like a Bible. By the time he returned to the sheriff, Tim was certain that's what it was. Tim stepped back and watched without a word as Bridger got on his knees beside the dying man and began to read over him.

At first the agent's voice was quavering, uncertain. Gradually, however, it gained resonance and power. Color flowed back into Bridger's face and Tim found himself thinking that if religious fervor alone could bring a man back from the brink, Bridger might save Turner after all.

Tim returned to Marylou and mounted the horse he had ridden to Moses's cabin, dropping Slade's carbine into the sleeve. Marylou mounted Bridger's horse and they rode back down the arroyo together. The last thing they heard as they cleared the arroyo was Bridger's powerful voice imploring God to look down in pity and compassion at this poor fallen creature at his feet.

Marylou was ahead of him as they rode out of the narrow draw about an hour later. He saw her dismount, look quickly about, then back at him in evident confusion.

"What's wrong?" he asked, as he rode up beside her and dismounted.

"Moses is not here! His body is gone!"

Tim looked around around the ledge, then down at the spot on the ground Marylou was staring at. Moses had been there, all right. There was a dark, rust-colored stain on a flat rock poking half out of the sand. Looking closer, he made out the faint imprint of a heavy body in the sand and around it the footprints of many moccasins.

Apache moccasins. The Apaches were back and they had taken Moses with them.

"Do you think he is alive?" Marylou asked hopefully.

Tim considered the odds. During the ride back to this spot, Marylou had told Tim how Moses had led them all into the narrow draw they had just passed through in order to give Moses and her a chance to break away. Marylou had not seen Moses shot, so she had not been able to tell Tim how badly he was hurt. There was a chance, then, that Moses—though left for dead—might still be alive, that the Apaches were taking care of him.

Yet when Tim glanced back at the blood stain on the ground and realized how much blood it would have

taken to leave that large a stain, he found he had little
real hope that Moses had survived.

"Tim!"

He glanced up.

An Apache had stepped from the rocks to his right.
He stood looking at them impassively. Another
stepped into view, then another. The Apaches began to
materialize from the rocks as if by magic until there
were close to a dozen silent Apaches surrounding
them.

Tim recognized two of the Indians at once. The first
one to appear, the tall Apache with the white headband
and the piercing blue eyes was Naretena, Tim realized
now. The other one he recognized was smaller, much
darker, his physique on an entirely different scale from
that of the broad-chested Apaches standing around
him. This was the medicine man who had saved Tim's
life. A Zuni, Moses had suggested.

The old Zuni stepped closer and peered up at Tim
with bright black eyes. "The One Who Moves
Mountains has returned," he said, his voice a dusty
whisper, his wrinkled lips parting in a gaping smile.
Then he looked down at Tim's feet. They were still
wrapped in pieces of his shirt and in some places dried
blood showed through. Tim had had some trouble
fitting his oversized feet into the stirrups. "You run like
a tired Apache on feet wrapped in rags," the Zuni said.
"We should call you One Who Runs on Bloody Feet."
He laughed. It sounded as dry as leaves scraping across
rocks. Then he turned to an Apache standing behind
him. The Apache stepped forward and handed the
Zuni a pair of moccasins. "Here," the Zuni said. "Wear
these."

Tim smiled and patiently unwrapped his feet, then
pulled the moccasins on. They fitted perfectly. "My

feet sing the praises of the soft buckskin," Tim told the Zuni. "Thank you."

The Zuni nodded, satisfied.

Naretena said something in Apache. The medicine man quickly stepped away from Tim. Naretena approached, regarding Marylou with intense interest. When he was close enough, he spoke to her, a curious warmth in his voice. "It is good the evil spirits brought by the *rurales* have gone from the golden one's head. The fear no longer clouds her eyes. They look out now and see the world. They show anger. They weep. They will laugh too. White Beard has done well."

"Where is White Beard?" Tim asked. "Where have you taken him?"

Naretena turned to Tim, a sadness in his face. "White Beard is dead," he said, his voice a little high and curiously strident. "The White Eyes he led to this place shot him. Why did old White Beard bring these men here? White Beard promised he would never come again to the People's mountain. His tongue was straight. Why did he come at last?"

"Those men made him," Tim told Naretena. "They wanted the gold Bart Talbot hid here in a mine shaft before the Apache arrow killed him."

Naretena nodded grimly and then stepped closer to Tim. "It is gone. The hole in the mountain has been closed. Do you not remember, One Who Moves Mountains?"

Tim frowned and looked at the Zuni. The man's sudden stump-toothed smile shook loose a host of dim memories. Even so, Tim was still unable to remember exactly what Naretena was referring to.

The Zuni stepped forward. "In the night," he told Tim, "when you joined our warriors and called out to the White Painted Woman and Child of Water—when you called your magic from the heavens and tore the mountain loose and sent great pieces of it down to cover the hole White Beard dug, do you not remember this? We danced until the stars fled. That night your medicine was powerful."

Tim remembered now. The confusion of images became clear at last. Tim felt again the ledge trembling under him as the great boulder crashed down into the night. And it told him what must have happened earlier when Moses pulled up in front of what should have been an open mine shaft and found it gone completely. It was then, perhaps, that he had decided to make his break for it—only to die in the attempt.

Tim looked at the Zuni and nodded. "Your medicine, too, is powerful." Then Tim turned back to Naretena. "Others will come for that gold. It belongs to Wells, Fargo."

Naretena frowned. "And who is this Wells, Fargo?"

"Wells, Fargo is the company of men that send their stagecoaches through the Devil's Playground on their way to California."

Naretena nodded. "Tell this Wells, Fargo that Naretena will keep the yellow bricks. He thanks Wells, Fargo. With these bricks of gold he can buy from the Comancheros the wagon guns, many rifles, the bullets with the brass jackets. The hole in the mountain is closed. That is true. But the Apache has taken the gold and will use it as the White Eyes use it. It will last many moons and already it brings many Apaches to stand beside Naretena."

"But that gold belongs to Wells, Fargo."

"It belongs to the People. It is from the Apache's mountains the gold comes. Now Wells, Fargo brings it back to us." He smiled at Tim. "It is a gift to the People for letting them go through the Apache's land."

"But you wipe out the Wells, Fargo stations, kill the station masters, run off their horses."

Naretena shook his head vigorously. "No. Apaches do not do this. It is Bart Talbot who killed and burned his own people. He kill many White Eyes so pony soldiers think it Apache."

Tim took a deep breath. Of course. That was all a part of it. How many of Bart Talbot's raises and assorted depredations had been blamed on the Apaches over the years? And this gold shipment. After Bridger had met with Bart and disappeared with the gold, his disappearance—along with the raise—might easily have been blamed on the Apaches.

"I would like to see now to White Beard's burial," Tim said. "Would you bring me to him?"

Naretena looked at the Zuni, who answered Tim. "White Beard has been buried by his brothers, the Apache. He lies now in a cave sealed with mud and great stones. No White Eyes and no Apache will disturb his sleep. Apaches are even now burning his lodge. It is done."

Naretena spoke then. "White Beard was the Apache's friend. My sorrow is as big as the earth. The golden headed one tried to avenge White Beard's death. She failed. But the Apache will see to it for her. There is one who is gone already from the canyon. Will the One Who Moves Mountains see to him?"

Naretena was undoubtedly referring to Slade. Tim nodded, wondering at the same time what the Apache had in mind for Bridger and the sheriff.

"Good," said Naretena. "I am content. Leave the Golden Mountain. It shall bleed no more for the White Eyes. Tell this to all the other White Eyes. But for you—the friend of White Beard, the One Who Moves

Mountains—there will be bricks of gold. How many will you take back with you?"

"None. It is the Apache's gold, after all. There is already too much blood on it."

"I do not understand. All White Eyes go crazy for gold. Even White Beard have the gold sickness."

"Like you, Naretena, my sorrow for the death of White Beard is as great as the earth. The blood of White Beard is on that gold—and many others as well. It would give me no pleasure to use that gold. While I spent it, I would think of White Beard and the others. Bad medicine, Naretena."

Naretena nodded once, sharply. He understood. "Then go. The Apache will escort you from this land in peace."

Tim turned from Naretena and helped Marylou mount up, then mounted himself. Tim's horse, nervous in the presence of the Indians, acted a little skittish. Tim leaned over to settle it down with a gentle pat on the neck, and when he looked up the Apaches were gone.

He pulled his horse around and led Marylou back out through the draw.

They found a hollow-eyed, strangely subdued Wells, Fargo agent still kneeling by the sheriff's side. He stood as Tim and Marylou rode up.

"The sheriff is dead," Bridger said. "A victim of God's wrath."

"Yes," Tim said, "and his own actions as well." Tim studied the agent. "Haven't you . . . changed your tune, somewhat, Bridger?"

The man's lean face took on a lugubriously melancholy cast. He raised his long arms suddenly over his head, his large, expressive hands opening up in a supplication to the heavens. "For too long have I listened to the seductive voice of Satan! Jesus!" the man cried. "Save me!"

Like tiny black thunderbolts, two Apache arrows appeared suddenly in Bridger's back, the sound they made as they plunged out of the sky like the whisper of wings. Another arrow plunged into the already-dead sheriff's chest. A third arrow sank into Bridger's back as the agent toppled forward onto his knees, then collapsed face down in the sand, his arms still spread wide. Another arrow buried itself in the sheriff's still form. As abruptly as it began, the lethal black shower ended.

Marylou had averted her face when the first Apache arrows struck Bridger.

"Let's ride out of here now, Marylou," Tim suggested gently. "We have a long ride ahead of us and night is coming on."

He started up, perfectly willing to leave the horse and the mules to the Apaches. Without a word, Marylou followed him.

Tim let her overtake him and drift into the lead. He did not look back at the two men and he was glad that Marylou did not either. The tracks were easy enough to follow and before sunset they passed the sad dark plume of smoke that came from Moses Kelly's burning cabin off to their left.

Tim heard a distant rifle shot and looked back.

Outlined against the red-streaked sky, he saw perhaps twenty-five to thirty Apaches atop a ridge. He waved. Gleaming Winchesters in their hands, the Apaches waved back; then, almost as a man, they vanished from sight.

As Tim rode into the gathering darkness, he remembered his promise to Naretena—to see to Slade Parkhurst.

It was a promise he intended to keep.

12

IT WAS LATE IN the day when Tim rode into Placerville a week later. He had left Marylou behind in Twin Forks with most of what was left of the money Bridger had given him.

The mining town was in its usual uproar with draymen cursing their overloaded teams, carriages clogging the streets, miners and assorted types swarming in and out of the saloons. No one took special notice of him when he rode up to the Wells, Fargo office and put his horse up to the hitch rail. As he dismounted and dropped the reins over the rail, Cass appeared in the office doorway.

"Afternoon, Cass," Tim said to the astonished fellow.

Cass was no longer wearing the somewhat ludicrous bowler. He was dressed in clean pants and vest, a white shirt of good quality broadcloth under it. He stood a mite taller also, it seemed. But his astonishment at seeing Tim was as genuine and youthful as ever.

"Mr. Bolton!"

"That's right, Cass. In the flesh. I keep turning up, don't I. Is there a Silas Wortham about?"

"The Pinkerton?"

"That's the fellow."

"He's across the street at the barbers."

"Get him for me, will you, Cass? I'll mind the store for you."

"Sure, Mr. Bolton. Sure."

As Cass darted across the street, Tim entered the office and found a chair. Once he had reached Twin Forks a week ago, he had telegraphed Wells, Fargo headquarters in San Francisco, advising them to have someone meet him in Placerville within a week if they wanted information concerning the lost gold shipment. A return telegram had informed him that a Pinkerton agent, by the name of Silas Wortham, would meet him at the Wells, Fargo office in Placerville in a week. Tim was keeping that appointment now.

A short stocky fellow with long sideburns and a thick, bushy mustache strode in ahead of Cass in less than five minutes. He was dressed in a fine pin-striped suit and a narrow-brimmed fedora. His pants legs were stuffed carelessly into beautifully-tooled boots and a wide cartridge belt circled his ample gut, the narrow-butt of a British Trantor poking out of his flapless holster. The Pinkerton was obviously not on an undercover mission.

Tim got to his feet and introduced himself. The Pinkerton shook his hand heartily. As Cass started to leave, Tim told him to stay. Wortham shrugged and sat himself down behind the big desk.

"All right, mister," Wortham said, thumbing his fedora back on his head. "What do you have to tell me concerning that gold shipment?"

"Wells, Fargo will never see it again."

"That so."

"That is so. Your agent here, Bridger, is dead. He conspired with Bart Talbot to rob the shipment. Slade Parkhurst, a local gambler, and the sheriff were in it with him."

"That's quite a gang."

"Bridger was not very smart."

"No. If you say so. How do you know all this, Bolton?"

"I was riding shotgun when Talbot raised the stage. I saw him and his men go directly to the gold as soon as they had stopped the stage. They were ripping up the floorboards in no time. They knew precisely where to look for it. They had even brought four mules with them to haul the gold off with."

"Interesting. Anything else?"

"A whiskey drummer was on that stage. The sheriff had lost a considerable amount to him. This was the way the sheriff paid him off."

Wortham took a deep breath, his beefy face suddenly pale. "That was no drummer. That was Carl Renstadt—a Pinkerton agent. He was onto something, he told me in a letter. But he didn't mention what."

That was a surprise to Tim. But it made sense, all right.

"Where's the gold now, Bolton?"

"The Apaches have it." Tim smiled slightly. "Their chief, Naretena, would like me to thank Wells, Fargo for returning the gold to him. He accepts it as a gift—and as payment for letting Wells, Fargo use that route through the Devil's Playground."

"Let us use it! Why he's been burning stations, terrorizing station masters. Do you know how many horses he has run off in a year?"

"That was Bart Talbot's work. It gave Bridger a fine

excuse for waiting until there was a sizable amount of gold to be shipped at one time. It is easy to blame everything on the Apache in this country."

"You mean this harrassment of our route through that country will stop? The Apaches will not bother us?"

Tim nodded.

"Well, damn it, that's good news, at least." Wortham smiled. "This Apache has the gold, you say?"

"That's right."

"I didn't think Apaches knew what to do with the stuff."

"This one does. He is buying weapons."

Wortham's eyebrows went up a notch. "That so? Well, he's welcome to that gold, I'd wager, if he keeps his promise."

"He will."

Tim finished up then by telling the Pinkerton about the deaths of the sheriff and Bridger. He saw no need to mention Moses Kelly or Marylou and left it to the Pinkerton's imagination to explain how Tim had become Naretena's spokesman in his dealings with Wells, Fargo.

When Tim got up to leave, Wortham said, "What about this Slade Parkhurst you say was in this with Bridger? Can you give me any evidence that will enable me to pull him in?"

"None."

The man frowned. "That's a damn shame."

"Leave him to me," Tim said quietly. Turning to Cass, who had listened to all this without a murmur, Tim asked, "Where is Slade now, Cass? The Miner's Haven?"

"Last I knew, Mr. Bolton."

"Just a minute, Mr. Bolton," said Wortham. "How do I know all this is as you say it is? Mind you, it all adds up. We had been getting a little wary of Bridger. But how do I know Naretena is really the one who has all that gold?"

"You don't. I'll be on my way back to Texas soon. When I get there I'll be taking over my grandfather's ranch, most likely. If the place starts blooming with expensive stock, new carriages, an addition to the ranchhouse—then I guess you'll know where I got the money."

"You can bet we'll be checking that out, Bolton."

"I expect you will. Good afternoon, Mr. Wortham."

Tim tugged his hat down firmly and strode out the door.

When Cass had gone to the barber shop for the Pinkerton agent, he had not been able to keep his voice low enough to prevent the barber from realizing that Tim Bolton had finally showed up. As the Pinkerton hurriedly left, the barber lost no time in relating this news to a few favored loungers outside his place of business; and in a matter of minutes, the sensational news was brought to the Miner's Haven.

Ronnie Gilbert, a small, wiry fellow who affected a crooked, ingratiating smile at all signs of trouble and who had lost more than his share at Slade's poker table, was the one who hastened to Slade's side to give him the news.

Slade didn't bother to thank the man or even acknowledge that he had heard him. He simply continued to study his hand. He had just drawn two jacks to give him—along with the one he had palmed—a full house, jacks and tens. He glanced idly across the table at Jacob Reddy, a miner who had already blown most of the dust he had brought in with him the day before.

The miner was the only player still in the game. He squinted unhappily at his cards, then bet. Slade raised him coldly, doubling his previous bet. The miner was trapped. He looked helplessly about, then pushed what few chips he had left into the pot.

"I'll owe you," the miner grumbled.

"Yes, you will," said Slade. "You calling?"

"What's it look like?"

Slade showed his full house. The miner slapped his own hand down in disgust.

Slade waved to the barkeep. "Cash me in," he called.

"Hey," the miner protested, "you gotta let me win some of that back."

Slade did not bother to reply to the miner as he got to his feet and walked to the bar. As the miner got up to pursue Slade, two men grabbed him from behind, sat him back down in his chair, and whispered anxiously into his ear. The miner quieted at once, then looked sheepishly about him at a remarkably hushed saloon.

Slade had watched it all by keeping his eye on the mirror behind the bar. Yes, everyone in the place knew that Bolton had finally shown. And now they were waiting. Slade hated to give them what they lusted after—and yet this had been coming since that day, more than a month ago, when he had gone after Amos Bruder. He had tried to avoid a confrontation then for the same reason that he feared one now. He was afraid of the Texan.

It was fear that had caused him to bolt in the canyon, almost running his horse into the ground in his frantic need to escape. It was that same fear that told him there was no place he could go to escape the Texan.

Bolton was like a curse, a nemesis that would never rest.

At the same time, Bolton was a man like any other—and just as mortal. It would not take a silver bullet to kill him. Just one well-placed round from Slade's revolver could do it.

And yet the man was his better. In him Slade saw again the incorruptible force that once he might have been—his fallen self. Slade frowned, ordered a whiskey, and then when it came, decided against drinking it. He was thinking like a romantic fool. He had only to face this the way he faced any simple game of poker—by leaving nothing to chance.

He felt better at once. He tossed down the whiskey and looked about him at the silent, hushed faces now watching him furtively. Yes, that was it. He would leave nothing to chance.

"Drinks on me!" Slade cried to the astonished crowd.

At first the men did not know whether or not to believe him. He saw the uncertainty on their faces and smiled around at them.

"What's the matter? You lost your thirst all of a sudden?"

With a roar the men rushed the bar. Slade buying! It was unheard of, and they intended to make the most of it. As the men jockeyed for places at the bar, Slade beckoned over one of the barkeep's assistants and told him to keep the liquor flowing until his day's winnings had been exhausted. With a nod, he indicated the pile of chips at his table.

He watched them for a moment. Like swine at the

trough, he said to himself and stepped from the saloon and headed for the blacksmith shop. Standish was still the acting sheriff.

And more anxious than ever to prove himself.

Tim noticed with grim amusement the way the streets and sidewalks of Placerville had grown quieter, more watchful. Those few he met as he strode along the boardwalk to the Miner's Haven swiftly averted their gaze and proceeded to look nervously about them for holes into which they might fly at a moment's notice.

When Tim saw the husky, black-browed fellow advancing diagonally across the street toward him, he at first paid him no heed—until he saw the dusty star pinned to his bib overalls, and the newly-polished ivory handled Colt swelling his holster.

Tim stopped and watched as the man walked closer. When the fellow was close enough for Tim to see that the star was that of a deputy, he understood. In Sheriff Turner's absence, this man had taken over. And now he wanted to prove that he deserved the job permanently.

Tim left the boardwalk to meet him. The apprentice lawman stopped then.

"You're under arrest, Bolton," the man said.

"What's your name?"

"My name's Standish. I'm the blacksmith in this town. But I've been the deputy while the sheriff took after you." He smiled. "Looks like I'll be the one to haul you in."

"What's the charge, deputy?"

"Murder."

"Who did I murder?"

"Amos Bruder."

"Do you have proof, deputy? Witnesses? Who is preferring the charges?"

The man looked suddenly uncomfortable.

Tim smiled thinly. "Is Slade Parkhurst your witness? Is it he that is preferring the charges?"

The deputy appeared to hesitate. Then he nodded grudgingly. "You must want to keep that star awful bad, Standish."

The man's eyes narrowed as he prepared a proper retort. Suddenly, however, they widened in surprise and dismay as he caught sight of something behind Tim, something he had not counted on. Tim needed no further warning. Cursing himself for his carelessness, he dove to his right and flung himself flat, his right hand clawing for leather. The shot came the instant he flung himself aside.

Even as he drew his weapon, he saw the deputy clutch his thigh and pitch forward. The bullet that had been meant for Tim had found the deputy instead. Tim flung himself around as another shot exploded the dirt in front of his face. Slade was standing at the head of an alley that had opened onto the street behind him and was coolly firing down at Tim.

Tim rolled over as another shot skinned his thigh. Then he charged to his feet and bolted up onto the boardwalk, cutting off the gambler's clear view of him. Flattening himself against the building, he heard feet racing down the alley. He flung himself around the corner of the building in time to see Slade disappear into a back alley.

Tim raced back onto the boardwalk, pelted along for at least three places of business, then barged through a narrow, mean-spirited saloon and out the back door. Slade was just ahead of him running down the back alley, heading for the rear of the livery stable.

Tim planted his feet firmly, aimed carefully, and fired at the retreating gambler. Slade stumbled forward, lost his footing, then regained his feet and darted into the stable.

Tim ran after him into the stable, his gun out and held ready. Within a couple of feet of a horse stall, Tim heard movement and pulled up. Slade straightened and walked slowly from it toward Tim. His face was white with pain. From the amount of blood staining the man's shirt, Tim guessed that the bullet had entered high up on the man's back. Slade still held his gun.

"Drop it, Slade," Tim said, aware for the first time that his own thigh was heavy with blood.

"You've blown out my back. I'm a dead man. You can't touch me now. I am not afraid of you anymore."

Slade brought up his six-gun. Tim fired from his hip. The slug entered Slade's chest, punching a darker hole in his already dark shirtfront. The force of the round slammed Slade back into the stall. Sitting down on a damp pile of straw and manure, Slade began to bring his gun up a second time. Tim leveled his gun swiftly, sighted down the barrel, thumbcocked, and fired. This bullet caught Slade in the chest again and slammed his head back against the wall.

A surprised look came into Slade's face; but with a massive, dogged insistence, he stumbled forward out of the stall and tried for the third time to bring up his revolver. Tim knocked the gun from his hand with one single sweep of his own six-gun.

Slade collapsed forward, turning slowly. He was bleeding at the mouth now, his dark eyes terrible with the fear of death in them. He landed on his knees, then pitched forward, flat on his face in the fresh muck of the stable, a buzzing swarm of fat blue flies already singing about his head.

Tim lifted the man over with the toe of his boot. As Slade flopped over, his sightless eyes staring up at Tim, blood-stained playing cards spilled out of a special pocket sewn into his vest. The man lay in the midst of aces and jacks and kings and queens, revealing at last in death what he had been all his life—a fourflusher and a cheat.

Tim became aware of men running into the stable and pressing close about him to get a better view of the body. Tim turned and pushed roughly through them and out of the place, striding along purposefully, refusing to reply to those who insisted on congratulating him, anxious only to rid himself of the stench of death.

As soon as Tim was solid in his saddle, he waved to the Pinkerton sitting in the Wells, Fargo doorway beside Cass and then looked down at the deputy. The man was leaning on a crutch, but it had not really hampered his blacksmithing.

"You sure there's no law against letting an Apache save my life?" Tim asked the deputy.

"I'm sure of it."

"And you saw Parkhurst shoot at me first."

Standish nodded ruefully.

"Good. I'm riding out of here and I don't want to have to look back."

Standish nodded soberly and moved away. Tim gave his horse a nudge and rode down the street and out of the town. He was as good as his word. He did not look back.

He was looking forward to Texas instead and to

maybe finding a home for Marylou with his grand-mother while he settled into work at the big panhandle spread. Maybe later, he and Marylou might . . . But he would not think of that now. The important thing was that both of them see to the task of banishing the ghosts of the past, that they begin over again.

That old medicine man may not really have spoken with his father as he had told Tim he had, but he sure as hell had given Tim good advice, and his heart was listening. His father was dead. It hadn't been Tim's fault. He should get on with his life now—just as his father would have wanted. It was his father, after all, who had seen to it that he did have this life.

When Tim was within a few miles of Twin Forks, he glanced to his right and caught a glimpse of the Devil's Playground, a dim jumble of peaks and towering buttes lying like wreckage on the horizon. He remembered then that line of Apache warriors silhouetted against the bright sky, their Winchesters gleaming in the setting sun.

Those Apaches would be a long time coming to heel. Their Golden Mountain would see to that. Tim was pleased at the thought.